Stolen Treasure

by

Howard Pyle

Stolen Treasure
by Howard Pyle

ISBN: 978-93-67146-26-2

Published by

DOUBLE 9 BOOKS

2/13-B, Ansari Road
Daryaganj, New Delhi – 110002
info@double9books.com
www.double9books.com
Tel. 011-40042856

ABOUT THE AUTHOR

Howard Pyle was an American artist who paints, draws, and writes books, mostly for kids. He was born March 5, 1853, and died November 9, 1911. In the last year of his life, he lived in Florence, Italy. He was born in Wilmington, Delaware. He began teaching drawing at the Drexel Institute of Art, Science, and Industry in 1894. This school is now called Drexel University. Violet Oakley, Maxfield Parrish, and Jessie Willcox Smith were pupils of his. He opened his own art and illustration school after 1900. It was called the Howard Pyle School of Illustration Art. After some time, scholar Henry C. Pitz used the name "Brandywine School" to refer to the illustration artists and Wyeth family artists who worked in the Brandywine area. Some of these artists had studied with Pyle. He shaped many artists who went on to become famous in their own right, including N. C. Wyeth, Frank Schoonover, Thornton Oakley, Allen Tupper True, Stanley Arthurs, and many more. Bill Pyle and Margaret Churchman Painter had a boy named Pyle. He was born in Wilmington, Delaware. He went to special schools as a child and liked drawing and writing from a very young age.

CONTENTS

I
WITH THE BUCCANEERS

Being an Account of Certain Adventures that Befell Henry Mostyn under Captain H. Morgan in the Year 1665-66.

I

Although this narration has more particularly to do with the taking of the Spanish Vice-Admiral in the harbor of Puerto Bello, and of the rescue therefrom of Le Sieur Simon, his wife and daughter (the adventure of which was successfully achieved by Captain Morgan, the famous buccaneer), we shall, nevertheless, premise something of the earlier history of Master Harry Mostyn, whom you may, if you please, consider as the hero of the several circumstances recounted in these pages.

In the year 1664 our hero's father embarked from Portsmouth, in England, for the Barbadoes, where he owned a considerable sugar plantation. Thither to those parts of America he transported with himself his whole family, of whom our Master Harry was the fifth of eight children—a great lusty fellow as little fitted for the Church (for which he was designed) as could be. At the time of this story, though not above sixteen years old, Master Harry Mostyn was as big and well-grown as many a man of twenty, and of such a reckless and dare-devil spirit that no adventure was too dangerous or too mischievous for him to embark upon.

At this time there was a deal of talk in those parts of the Americas concerning Captain Morgan, and the prodigious successes he was having pirating against the Spaniards.

This man had once been an indentured servant with Mr. Rolls, a sugar factor at the Barbadoes. Having served out his time, and being of lawless disposition, possessing also a prodigious appetite for adventure, he joined with others of his kidney, and, purchasing a caraval of three guns, embarked fairly upon that career of piracy the most successful that ever was heard of in the world.

Master Harry had known this man very well while he was still with Mr. Rolls, serving as a clerk at that gentleman's sugar wharf, a tall, broad-shouldered, strapping fellow, with red cheeks, and thick red lips, and rolling blue eyes, and hair as red as any chestnut. Many knew him for a bold, gruff-spoken man, but no one at that time suspected that he had it in him to become so famous and renowned as he afterwards grew to be.

The fame of his exploits had been the talk of those parts for above a twelvemonth, when, in the latter part of the year 1665, Captain Morgan, having made a very successful expedition against the Spaniards into the Gulf of Campeachy—where he took several important purchases from the plate fleet—came to the Barbadoes, there to fit out another such venture, and to enlist recruits.

He and certain other adventurers had purchased a vessel of some five hundred tons, which they proposed to convert into a pirate by cutting port-holes for cannon, and running three or four carronades across her main-deck. The name of this ship, be it mentioned, was the *Good Samaritan*, as ill-fitting a name as could be for such a craft, which, instead of being designed for the healing of wounds, was intended to inflict such devastation as those wicked men proposed.

Here was a piece of mischief exactly fitted to our hero's tastes; wherefore, having made up a bundle of clothes, and with not above a shilling in his pocket, he made an excursion into the town to seek for Captain Morgan. There he found the great pirate established at an ordinary, with a little court of ragamuffins and swashbucklers gathered about him, all talking very loud, and drinking healths in raw rum as though it were sugared water.

And what a fine figure our buccaneer had grown, to be sure! How different from the poor, humble clerk upon the sugarwharf! What a deal of gold braid! What a fine, silver-hilted Spanish sword! What a gay velvet sling, hung with three silver-mounted pistols! If Master Harry's mind had not been made up before, to be sure such a spectacle of glory would have determined it.

This figure of war our hero asked to step aside with him, and when they had come into a corner, proposed to the other what he intended, and that he had a mind to enlist as a gentleman adventurer upon this expedition. Upon this our rogue of a buccaneer Captain burst out a-laughing, and fetching Master Harry a great thump upon the back, swore roundly that he would make a man of him, and that it was a pity to make a parson out of so good a piece of stuff.

"THIS FIGURE OF WAR OUR HERO ASKED TO STEP ASIDE WITH HIM"

Nor was Captain Morgan less good than his word, for when the *Good Samaritan* set sail with a favoring wind for the island of Jamaica, Master Harry found himself established as one of the adventurers aboard.

II

Could you but have seen the town of Port Royal as it appeared in the year 1665 you would have beheld a sight very well worth while looking upon. There were no fine houses at that time, and no great counting-houses built of brick, such as you may find nowadays, but a crowd of board and wattled huts huddled along the streets, and all so gay with flags and bits of color that Vanity Fair itself could not have been gayer. To this place came all the pirates and buccaneers that infested those parts, and men shouted and swore and gambled, and poured out money like water, and then maybe wound up their merrymaking by dying of fever. For the sky in these torrid latitudes is all full of clouds overhead, and as hot as any blanket, and when the sun shone forth it streamed down upon the smoking sands so that the houses were ovens and the streets were furnaces; so it was little wonder that men died like rats in a hole. But little they appeared to care for that; so that everywhere you might behold a multitude of painted women and Jews and merchants and pirates, gaudy with red scarfs and gold braid and all sorts of odds and ends of foolish finery, all fighting and gambling and bartering for that ill-gotten treasure of the be-robbed Spaniard.

Here, arriving, Captain Morgan found a hearty welcome, and a message from the Governor awaiting him, the message bidding him attend his Excellency upon the earliest occasion that offered. Whereupon, taking our hero (of whom he had grown prodigiously fond) along with him, our pirate went, without any loss of time, to visit Sir Thomas Modiford, who was then the royal Governor of all this devil's brew of wickedness.

They found his Excellency seated in a great easy-chair, under the shadow of a slatted veranda, the floor whereof was paved with brick. He was clad, for the sake of coolness, only in his shirt, breeches, and stockings, and he wore slippers on his feet. He was smoking a great cigarro of tobacco, and a goblet of lime-juice and water and rum stood at his elbow on a table. Here, out of the glare of the heat, it was all very cool and pleasant, with a sea-breeze blowing violently in through the slats, setting them a-rattling now and then, and stirring Sir Thomas's long hair, which he had pushed back for the sake of coolness.

The purport of this interview, I may tell you, concerned the rescue of one Le Sieur Simon, who, together with his wife and daughter, was held captive by the Spaniards.

This gentleman adventurer (Le Sieur Simon) had, a few years before, been set up by the buccaneers as Governor of the island of Santa Catherina. This place, though well fortified by the Spaniards, the buccaneers had seized upon, establishing themselves thereon, and so infesting the commerce of those seas that no Spanish fleet was safe from them. At last the Spaniards, no longer able to endure these assaults against their commerce, sent a great force against the freebooters to drive them out of their island stronghold. This they did, retaking Santa Catherina, together with its Governor, his wife, and daughter, as well as the whole garrison of buccaneers.

This garrison were sent by their conquerors, some to the galleys, some to the mines, some to no man knows where. The Governor himself—Le Sieur Simon—was to be sent to Spain, there to stand his trial for piracy.

The news of all this, I may tell you, had only just been received in Jamaica, having been brought thither by a Spanish captain, one Don Roderiguez Sylvia, who was, besides, the bearer of despatches to the Spanish authorities relating the whole affair.

Such, in fine, was the purport of this interview, and as our hero and his Captain walked back together from the Governor's house to the ordinary where they had taken up their inn, the buccaneer assured his companion that he purposed to obtain those despatches from the Spanish captain that very afternoon, even if he had to use force to seize them.

All this, you are to understand, was undertaken only because of the friendship that the Governor and Captain Morgan entertained for Le Sieur Simon. And, indeed, it was wonderful how honest and how faithful were these wicked men in their dealings with one another. For you must know that Governor Modiford and Le Sieur Simon and the buccaneers were all of one kidney—all taking a share in the piracies of those times, and all holding by one another as though they were the honestest men in the world. Hence it was they were all so determined to rescue Le Sieur Simon from the Spaniards.

III

Having reached his ordinary after his interview with the Governor, Captain Morgan found there a number of his companions, such as usually gathered at that place to be in attendance upon him—some, those belonging to the *Good Samaritan*; others, those who hoped to obtain benefits from him; others, those ragamuffins who gathered around him because he was famous, and because it pleased them to be of his court and to be called his followers. For nearly always your successful pirate had such a little court surrounding him.

Finding a dozen or more of these rascals gathered there, Captain Morgan informed them of his present purpose—that he was going to find the Spanish captain to demand his papers of him, and calling upon them to accompany him.

With this following at his heels, our buccaneer started off down the street, his lieutenant, a Cornishman named Bartholomew Davis, upon one hand and our hero upon the other. So they paraded the streets for the best part of an hour before they found the Spanish captain. For whether he had got wind that Captain Morgan was searching for him, or whether, finding himself in a place so full of his enemies, he had buried himself in some place of hiding, it is certain that the buccaneers had traversed pretty nearly the whole town before they discovered that he was lying at a certain auberge kept by a Portuguese Jew. Thither they went, and thither Captain Morgan entered with the utmost coolness and composure of demeanor, his followers crowding noisily in at his heels.

The space within was very dark, being lighted only by the doorway and by two large slatted windows or openings in the front.

In this dark, hot place—not over-roomy at the best—were gathered twelve or fifteen villanous-appearing men, sitting at tables and drinking together, waited upon by the Jew and his wife. Our hero had no trouble in discovering which of this lot of men was Captain Sylvia, for not only did Captain Morgan direct his glance full of war upon him, but the Spaniard was clad with more particularity and with more show of finery than any of the others who were there.

Him Captain Morgan approached and demanded his papers, whereunto the other replied with such a jabber of Spanish and English that no man could have understood what he said. To this Captain Morgan in turn replied that he must have those papers, no matter what it might cost him to obtain them, and thereupon drew a pistol from his sling and presented it at the other's head.

At this threatening action the innkeeper's wife fell a-screaming, and the Jew, as in a frenzy, besought them not to tear the house down about his ears.

Our hero could hardly tell what followed, only that all of a sudden there was a prodigious uproar of combat. Knives flashed everywhere, and then a pistol was fired so close to his head that he stood like one stunned, hearing some one crying out in a loud voice, but not knowing whether it was a friend or a foe who had been shot. Then another pistol-shot so deafened what was left of Master Harry's hearing that his ears rang for above an hour afterwards. By this time the whole place was full of gunpowder smoke, and there was the sound of blows and oaths and outcrying and the clashing of knives.

As Master Harry, who had no great stomach for such a combat, and no very particular interest in the quarrel, was making for the door, a little Portuguese, as withered and as nimble as an ape, came ducking under the table and plunged at his stomach with a great long knife, which, had it effected its object, would surely have ended his adventures then and there.

Finding himself in such danger, Master Harry snatched up a heavy chair, and, flinging it at his enemy, who was preparing for another attack, he fairly ran for it out of the door, expecting every instant to feel the thrust of the blade betwixt his ribs.

A considerable crowd had gathered outside, and others, hearing the uproar, were coming running to join them. With these our hero stood, trembling like a leaf, and with cold chills running up and down his back like water at the narrow escape from the danger that had threatened him.

Nor shall you think him a coward, for you must remember he was hardly sixteen years old at the time, and that this was the first affair of the sort he had encountered. Afterwards, as you shall learn, he showed that he could exhibit courage enough at a pinch.

While he stood there endeavoring to recover his composure, the while the tumult continued within, suddenly two men came running almost together out of the door, a crowd of the combatants at their heels. The first of these men was Captain Sylvia; the other, who was pursuing him, was Captain Morgan.

As the crowd about the door parted before the sudden appearing of these, the Spanish captain, perceiving, as he supposed, a way of escape opened to him, darted across the street with incredible swiftness towards an alleyway upon the other side. Upon this, seeing his prey like to get away from him, Captain Morgan snatched a pistol out of his sling, and resting it for an instant across his arm, fired at the flying Spaniard, and that with so true an aim that, though the street was now full of people, the other went tumbling over and over all of a heap in the kennel, where he lay, after a twitch or two, as still as a log.

At the sound of the shot and the fall of the man the crowd scattered upon all sides, yelling and screaming, and the street being thus pretty clear, Captain Morgan ran across the way to where his victim lay, his smoking pistol still in his hand, and our hero following close at his heels.

Our poor Harry had never before beheld a man killed thus in an instant who a moment before had been so full of life and activity, for when Captain Morgan turned the body over upon its back he could perceive at a glance, little as he knew of such matters, that the man was stone dead. And, indeed, it was a dreadful sight for him who was hardly more than a child. He stood rooted for he knew not how long, staring down at the dead face with twitching fingers and shuddering limbs. Meantime a great crowd was gathering about them again.

As for Captain Morgan, he went about his work with the utmost coolness and deliberation imaginable, unbuttoning the waistcoat and the shirt of the man he had murdered with fingers that neither twitched nor shook. There were a gold cross and a bunch of silver medals hung by a whip-cord about the neck of the dead man. This Captain Morgan broke away with a snap, reaching the jingling baubles to Harry, who took them in his nerveless hand and fingers that he could hardly close upon what they held.

The papers Captain Morgan found in a wallet in an inner breast-pocket of the Spaniard's waistcoat. These he examined one by one, and finding them to his satisfaction, tied them up again, and slipped the wallet and its contents into his own pocket.

Then for the first time he appeared to observe Master Harry, who, indeed, must have been standing the perfect picture of horror and dismay. Whereupon, bursting out a-laughing, and slipping the pistol he had used back into its sling again, he fetched poor Harry a great slap upon the back, bidding him be a man, for that he would see many such sights as this.

But, indeed, it was no laughing matter for poor Master Harry, for it was many a day before his imagination could rid itself of the image of the dead Spaniard's face; and as he walked away down the street with his companions, leaving the crowd behind them, and the dead body where it lay for its friends to look after, his ears humming and ringing from the deafening noise of the pistol-shots fired in the close room, and the sweat trickling down his face in drops, he knew not whether all that had passed had been real, or whether it was a dream from which he might presently awaken.

IV

The papers Captain Morgan had thus seized upon as the fruit of the murder he had committed must have been as perfectly satisfactory to him as could be, for having paid a second visit that evening to Governor Modiford, the pirate lifted anchor the next morning and made sail towards the Gulf of Darien. There, after cruising about in those waters for about a fortnight without falling in with a vessel of any sort, at the end of that time they overhauled a caravel bound from Puerto Bello to Cartagena, which vessel they took, and finding her loaded with nothing better than raw hides, scuttled and sunk her, being then about twenty leagues from the main of Cartagena. From the captain of this vessel they learned that the plate fleet was then lying in the harbor of Puerto Bello, not yet having set sail thence, but waiting for the change of the winds before embarking for Spain. Besides this, which was a good deal more to their purpose, the Spaniards told the pirates that the Sieur Simon, his wife, and daughter were confined aboard the vice-admiral of that fleet, and that the name of the vice-admiral was the *Santa Maria y Valladolid*.

So soon as Captain Morgan had obtained the information he desired he directed his course straight for the Bay of Santo Blaso, where he might lie safely within the cape of that name without any danger of discovery (that part of the main-land being entirely uninhabited) and yet be within twenty or twenty-five leagues of Puerto Bello.

Having come safely to this anchorage, he at once declared his intentions to his companions, which were as follows:

That it was entirely impossible for them to hope to sail their vessel into the harbor of Puerto Bello, and to attack the Spanish vice-admiral where he lay in the midst of the armed flota; wherefore, if anything was to be accomplished, it must be undertaken by some subtle design rather than by open-handed boldness. Having so prefaced what he had to say, he now declared that it was his purpose to take one of the ship's boats and to go in that to Puerto Bello, trusting for some opportunity to occur to aid him either in the accomplishment of his aims or in the gaining of some further information. Having thus delivered himself, he invited any who dared to do so to volunteer for the expedition, telling them plainly that he would constrain no man to go against his will, for that at best it was a desperate enterprise, possessing only the recommendation that in its achievement the few who undertook it would gain great renown, and perhaps a very considerable booty.

And such was the incredible influence of this bold man over his companions, and such was their confidence in his skill and cunning, that not above a dozen of all those aboard hung back from the undertaking, but nearly every man desired to be taken.

Of these volunteers Captain Morgan chose twenty—among others our Master Harry—and having arranged with his lieutenant that if nothing was heard from the expedition at the end of three days he should sail for Jamaica to await news, he embarked upon that enterprise, which, though never heretofore published, was perhaps the boldest and the most desperate of all those that have since made his name so famous. For what could be a more unparalleled undertaking than for a little open boat, containing but twenty men, to enter the harbor of the third strongest fortress of the Spanish mainland with the intention of cutting out the Spanish vice-admiral from the midst of a whole fleet of powerfully armed vessels, and how many men in all the world do you suppose would venture such a thing?

But there is this to be said of that great buccaneer: that if he undertook enterprises so desperate as this, he yet laid his plans so well that they never went altogether amiss. Moreover, the very desperation of his successes was of such a nature that no man could suspect that he would dare to undertake such things, and accordingly his enemies were never prepared to guard against his attacks. Aye, had he but worn the King's colors and served under the rules of honest war, he might have become as great and as renowned as Admiral Blake himself!

But all that is neither here nor there; what I have to tell you now is that Captain Morgan in this open boat with his twenty mates reached the Cape of Salmedina towards the fall of day. Arriving within view of the harbor they discovered the plate fleet at anchor, with two men-of-war and an armed galley riding as a guard at the mouth of the harbor, scarce half a league distant from the other ships. Having spied the fleet in this posture, the pirates presently pulled down their sails and rowed along the coast, feigning to be a Spanish vessel from Nombre de Dios. So hugging the shore, they came boldly within the harbor, upon the opposite side of which you might see the fortress a considerable distance away.

Being now come so near to the consummation of their adventure, Captain Morgan required every man to make an oath to stand by him to the last, whereunto our hero swore as heartily as any man aboard, although his heart, I must needs confess, was beating at a great rate at the approach of what was to happen. Having thus received the oaths of all his followers, Captain Morgan commanded the surgeon of the expedition that, when the order was given, he, the medico, was to bore six holes in the boat, so that, it sinking under them, they might all be compelled to push forward, with no chance of retreat. And such was the ascendency of this man over his followers, and such was their awe of him, that not one of them uttered even so much as a murmur, though what he had commanded the surgeon to do pledged them either to victory or to death, with no chance to choose between. Nor did the surgeon question the orders he had received, much less did he dream of disobeying them.

By now it had fallen pretty dusk, whereupon, spying two fishermen in a canoe at a little distance, Captain Morgan demanded of them in Spanish which vessel of those at anchor in the harbor was the vice-admiral, for that he had despatches for the captain thereof. Whereupon the fishermen, suspecting nothing, pointed to them a galleon of great size riding at anchor not half a league distant.

Towards this vessel accordingly the pirates directed their course, and when they had come pretty nigh, Captain Morgan called upon the surgeon that now it was time for him to perform the duty that had been laid upon him. Whereupon the other did as he was ordered, and that so thoroughly that the water presently came gushing into the boat in great streams, whereat all hands pulled for the galleon as though every next moment was to be their last.

And what do you suppose were our hero's emotions at this time? Like all in the boat, his awe of Captain Morgan was so great that I do believe he would rather have gone to the bottom than have questioned his command, even when it was to scuttle the boat. Nevertheless, when he felt the cold water gushing about his feet (for he had taken off his shoes and stockings) he became possessed with such a fear of being drowned that even the Spanish galleon had no terrors for him if he could only feel the solid planks thereof beneath his feet.

Indeed, all the crew appeared to be possessed of a like dismay, for they pulled at the oars with such an incredible force that they were under the quarter of the galleon before the boat was half filled with water.

Here, as they approached, it then being pretty dark and the moon not yet having risen, the watch upon the deck hailed them, whereupon Captain Morgan called out in Spanish that he was Captain Alvarez Mendazo, and that he brought despatches for the vice-admiral.

But at that moment, the boat being now so full of water as to be logged, it suddenly tilted upon one side as though to sink beneath them, whereupon all hands, without further orders, went scrambling up the side, as nimble as so many monkeys, each armed with a pistol in one hand and a cutlass in the other, and so were upon deck before the watch could collect his wits to utter any outcry or to give any other alarm than to cry out, "Jesu bless us! who are these?" at which words somebody knocked him down with the butt of a pistol, though who it was our hero could not tell in the darkness and the hurry.

Before any of those upon deck could recover from their alarm or those from below come up upon deck, a part of the pirates, under the carpenter and the surgeon, had run to the gunroom and had taken possession of the arms, while Captain Morgan, with Master Harry and a Portuguese called Murillo Braziliano, had flown with the speed of the wind into the great cabin.

Here they found the captain of the vice-admiral playing at cards with the Sieur Simon and a friend, Madam Simon and her daughter being present.

Captain Morgan instantly set his pistol at the breast of the Spanish captain, swearing with a most horrible fierce countenance that if he spake a word or made any outcry he was a dead man. As for our hero, having now got his hand into the game, he performed the same service for the Spaniard's friend, declaring he would shoot him dead if he opened his lips or lifted so much as a single finger.

All this while the ladies, not comprehending what had occurred, had sat as mute as stones; but now having so far recovered themselves as to find a voice, the younger of the two fell to screaming, at which the Sieur Simon called out to her to be still, for these were friends who had come to help them, and not enemies who had come to harm them.

All this, you are to understand, occupied only a little while, for in less than a minute three or four of the pirates had come into the cabin, who, together with the Portuguese, proceeded at once to bind the two Spaniards hand and foot, and to gag them. This being done to our buccaneer's satisfaction, and the Spanish captain being stretched out in the corner of the cabin, he instantly cleared his countenance of its terrors, and bursting forth into a great loud laugh, clapped his hand to the Sieur Simon's, which he wrung with the best will in the world. Having done this, and being in a fine humor after this his first success, he turned to the two ladies. "And this, ladies," said he, taking our hero by the hand and presenting him, "is a young gentleman who has embarked with me to learn the trade of piracy. I recommend him to your politeness."

Think what a confusion this threw our Master Harry into, to be sure, who at his best was never easy in the company of strange ladies! You may suppose what must have been his emotions to find himself thus introduced to the attention of Madam Simon and her daughter, being at the time in his bare feet, clad only in his shirt and breeches, and with no hat upon his head, a pistol in one hand and a cutlass in the other. However, he was not left for long to his embarrassments, for almost immediately after he had thus far relaxed, Captain Morgan fell of a sudden serious again, and bidding the Sieur Simon to get his ladies away into some place of safety, for the most hazardous part of this adventure was yet to occur, he quitted the cabin with Master Harry and the other pirates (for you may call him a pirate now) at his heels.

Having come upon deck, our hero beheld that a part of the Spanish crew were huddled forward in a flock like so many sheep (the others being crowded below with the hatches fastened upon them), and such was the terror of the pirates, and so dreadful the name of Henry Morgan, that not one of those poor wretches dared to lift up his voice to give any alarm, nor even to attempt an escape by jumping overboard.

At Captain Morgan's orders, these men, together with certain of his own company, ran nimbly aloft and began setting the sails, which, the night now having fallen pretty thick, was not for a good while observed by any of the vessels riding at anchor about them.

Indeed, the pirates might have made good their escape, with at most only a shot or two from the men-of-war, had it not then been about the full of the moon, which, having arisen, presently discovered to those of the fleet that lay closest about them what was being done aboard the vice-admiral.

At this one of the vessels hailed them, and then after a while, having no reply, hailed them again. Even then the Spaniards might not immediately have suspected anything was amiss but only that the vice-admiral for some reason best known to himself was shifting his anchorage, had not one of the Spaniards aloft—but who it was Captain Morgan was never able to discover—answered the hail by crying out that the vice-admiral had been seized by the pirates.

At this the alarm was instantly given and the mischief done, for presently there was a tremendous bustle through that part of the fleet lying nighest the vice-admiral—a deal of shouting of orders, a beating of drums, and the running hither and thither of the crews.

But by this time the sails of the vice-admiral had filled with a strong land breeze that was blowing up the harbor, whereupon the carpenter, at Captain Morgan's orders, having cut away both anchors, the galleon presently bore away up the harbor, gathering headway every moment with the wind nearly dead astern. The nearest vessel was the only one that for the moment was able to offer any hinderance. This ship, having by this time cleared away one of its guns, was able to fire a parting shot against the vice-admiral, striking her somewhere forward, as our hero could see by a great shower of splinters that flew up in the moonlight.

At the sound of the shot all the vessels of the flota not yet disturbed by the alarm were aroused at once, so that the pirates had the satisfaction of knowing that they would have to run the gantlet of all the ships between them and the open sea before they could reckon themselves escaped.

And, indeed, to our hero's mind it seemed that the battle which followed must have been the most terrific cannonade that was ever heard in the world. It was not so ill at first, for it was some while before the Spaniards could get their guns clear for action, they being not the least in the world prepared for such an occasion as this. But by-and-by first one and then another ship opened fire upon the galleon, until it seemed to our hero that all the thunders of heaven let loose upon them could not have created a more prodigious uproar, and that it was not possible that they could any of them escape destruction.

By now the moon had risen full and round, so that the clouds of smoke that rose in the air appeared as white as snow. The air seemed full of the hiss and screaming of shot, each one of which, when it struck the galleon, was magnified by our hero's imagination into ten times its magnitude from the crash which it delivered and from the cloud of splinters it would cast up into the moonlight. At last he suddenly beheld one poor man knocked sprawling across the deck, who, as he raised his arm from behind the mast, disclosed that the hand was gone from it, and that the shirt-sleeve was red with blood in the moonlight. At this sight all the strength fell away from poor Harry, and he felt sure that a like fate or even a worse must be in store for him.

But, after all, this was nothing to what it might have been in broad daylight, for what with the darkness of night, and the little preparation the Spaniards could make for such a business, and the extreme haste with which they discharged their guns (many not understanding what was the occasion of all this uproar), nearly all the shot flew so wide of the mark that not above one in twenty struck that at which it was aimed.

Meantime Captain Morgan, with the Sieur Simon, who had followed him upon deck, stood just above where our hero lay behind the shelter of the bulwark. The captain had lit a pipe of tobacco, and he stood now in the bright moonlight close to the rail, with his hands behind him, looking out ahead with the utmost coolness imaginable, and paying no more attention to the din of battle than though it were twenty leagues away. Now and then he would take his pipe from his lips to utter an order to the man at the wheel. Excepting this he stood there hardly moving at all, the wind blowing his long red hair over his shoulders.

Had it not been for the armed galley the pirates might have got the galleon away with no great harm done in spite of all this cannonading, for the man-of-war which rode at anchor nighest to them at the mouth of the harbor was still so far away that they might have passed it by hugging pretty close to the shore, and that without any great harm being done to them in the darkness. But just at this moment, when the open water lay in sight, came this galley pulling out from behind the point of the shore in such a manner as either to head our pirates off entirely or else to compel them to approach so near to the man-of-war that that latter vessel could bring its guns to bear with more effect.

This galley, I must tell you, was like others of its kind such as you may find in these waters, the hull being long and cut low to the water so as to allow the oars to dip freely. The bow was sharp and projected far out ahead, mounting a swivel upon it, while at the stern a number of galleries built one above another into a castle gave shelter to several companies of musketeers as well as the officers commanding them.

Our hero could behold the approach of this galley from above the starboard bulwarks, and it appeared to him impossible for them to hope to escape either it or the man-of-war. But still Captain Morgan maintained the same composure that he had exhibited all the while, only now and then delivering an order to the man at the wheel, who, putting the helm over, threw the bows of the galleon around more to the larboard, as though to escape the bow of the galley and get into the open water beyond. This course brought the pirates ever closer and closer to the man-of-war, which now began to add its thunder to the din of the battle, and with so much more effect that at every discharge you might hear the crashing and crackling of splintered wood, and now and then the outcry or groaning of some man who was hurt. Indeed, had it been daylight, they must at this juncture all have perished, though, as was said, what with the night and the confusion and the hurry, they escaped entire destruction, though more by a miracle than through any policy upon their own part.

Meantime the galley, steering as though to come aboard of them, had now come so near that it, too, presently began to open its musketry fire upon them, so that the humming and rattling of bullets were presently added to the din of cannonading.

In two minutes more it would have been aboard of them, when in a moment Captain Morgan roared out of a sudden to the man at the helm to put it hard a starboard. In response the man ran the wheel over with the utmost quickness, and the galleon, obeying her helm very readily, came around upon a course which, if continued, would certainly bring them into collision with their enemy.

It is possible at first the Spaniards imagined the pirates intended to escape past their stern, for they instantly began backing oars to keep them from getting past, so that the water was all of a foam about them; at the same time they did this they poured in such a fire of musketry that it was a miracle that no more execution was accomplished than happened.

As for our hero, methinks for the moment he forgot all about everything else than as to whether or no his captain's manoeuvre would succeed, for in the very first moment he divined, as by some instinct, what Captain Morgan purposed doing.

At this moment, so particular in the execution of this nice design, a bullet suddenly struck down the man at the wheel. Hearing the sharp outcry, our Harry turned to see him fall forward, and then to his hands and knees upon the deck, the blood running in a black pool beneath him, while the wheel, escaping from his hands, spun over until the spokes were all of a mist.

In a moment the ship would have fallen off before the wind had not our hero, leaping to the wheel (even as Captain Morgan shouted an order for some one to do so), seized the flying spokes, whirling them back again, and so bringing the bow of the galleon up to its former course.

"OUR HERO, LEAPING TO THE WHEEL, SEIZED THE FLYING SPOKES"

In the first moment of this effort he had reckoned of nothing but of carrying out his captain's designs. He neither thought of cannon-balls nor of bullets. But now that his task was accomplished, he came suddenly back to himself to find the galleries of the galleon aflame with musket-shots, and to become aware with a most horrible sinking of the spirits that all the shots therefrom were intended for him. He cast his eyes about him with despair, but no one came to ease him of his task, which, having undertaken, he had too much spirit to resign from carrying through to the end, though he was well aware that the very next instant might mean his sudden and violent death. His ears hummed and rang, and his brain swam as light as a feather. I know not whether he breathed, but he shut his eyes tight as though that might save him from the bullets that were raining about him.

At this moment the Spaniards must have discovered for the first time the pirates' design, for of a sudden they ceased firing, and began to shout out a multitude of orders, while the oars lashed the water all about with a foam. But it was too late then for them to escape, for within a couple of seconds the galleon struck her enemy a blow so violent upon the larboard quarter as nearly to hurl our Harry upon the deck, and then with a dreadful, horrible crackling of wood, commingled with a yelling of men's voices, the galley was swung around upon her side, and the galleon, sailing into the open sea, left nothing of her immediate enemy but a sinking wreck, and the water dotted all over with bobbing heads and waving hands in the moonlight.

And now, indeed, that all danger was past and gone, there were plenty to come running to help our hero at the wheel. As for Captain Morgan, having come down upon the main-deck, he fetches the young helmsman a clap upon the back. "Well, Master Harry," says he, "and did I not tell you I would make a man of you?" Whereat our poor Harry fell a-laughing, but with a sad catch in his voice, for his hands trembled as with an ague, and were as cold as ice. As for his emotions, God knows he was nearer crying than laughing, if Captain Morgan had but known it.

Nevertheless, though undertaken under the spur of the moment, I protest it was indeed a brave deed, and I cannot but wonder how many young gentlemen of sixteen there are to-day who, upon a like occasion, would act as well as our Harry.

V

The balance of our hero's adventures were of a lighter sort than those already recounted, for the next morning, the Spanish captain (a very polite and well-bred gentleman) having fitted him out with a suit of his own clothes, Master Harry was presented in a proper form to the ladies. For Captain Morgan, if he had felt a liking for the young man before, could not now show sufficient regard for him. He ate in the great cabin and was petted by all. Madam Simon, who was a fat and red-faced lady, was forever praising him, and the young miss, who was extremely well-looking, was as continually making eyes at him.

She and Master Harry, I must tell you, would spend hours together, she making pretence of teaching him French, although he was so possessed with a passion of love that he was nigh suffocated with it. She, upon her part, perceiving his emotions, responded with extreme good-nature and complacency, so that had our hero been older, and the voyage proved longer, he might have become entirely enmeshed in the toils of his fair siren. For all this while, you are to understand, the pirates were making sail straight for Jamaica, which they reached upon the third day in perfect safety.

"SHE AND MASTER HARRY WOULD SPEND HOURS TOGETHER"

In that time, however, the pirates had well-nigh gone crazy for joy; for when they came to examine their purchase they discovered her cargo to consist of plate to the prodigious sum of £130,000 in value. 'Twas a wonder they did not all make themselves drunk for joy. No doubt they would have done so had not Captain Morgan, knowing they were still in the exact track of the Spanish fleets, threatened them that the first man among them who touched a drop of rum without his permission he would shoot him dead upon the deck. This threat had such effect that they all remained entirely sober until they had reached Port Royal Harbor, which they did about nine o'clock in the morning.

And now it was that our hero's romance came all tumbling down about his ears with a run. For they had hardly come to anchor in the harbor when a boat came from a man-of-war, and who should come stepping aboard but Lieutenant Grantley (a particular friend of our hero's father) and his own eldest brother Thomas, who, putting on a very stern face, informed Master Harry that he was a desperate and hardened villain who was sure to end at the gallows, and that he was to go immediately back to his home again. He told our embryo pirate that his family had nigh gone distracted because of his wicked and ungrateful conduct. Nor could our hero move him from his inflexible purpose. "What," says our Harry, "and will you not then let me wait until our prize is divided and I get my share?"

"Prize, indeed!" says his brother. "And do you then really think that your father would consent to your having a share in this terrible bloody and murthering business?"

And so, after a good deal of argument, our hero was constrained to go; nor did he even have an opportunity to bid adieu to his inamorata. Nor did he see her any more, except from a distance, she standing on the poop-deck as he was rowed away from her, her face all stained with crying. For himself, he felt that there was no more joy in life; nevertheless, standing up in the stern of the boat, he made shift, though with an aching heart, to deliver her a fine bow with the hat he had borrowed from the Spanish captain, before his brother bade him sit down again.

And so to the ending of this story, with only this to relate, that our Master Harry, so far from going to the gallows, became in good time a respectable and wealthy sugar merchant with an English wife and a fine family of children, whereunto, when the mood was upon him, he has sometimes told these adventures (and sundry others not here recounted) as I have told them unto you.

II
TOM CHIST AND THE TREASURE-BOX

An Old-time Story of the Days of Captain Kidd.

To tell about Tom Chist, and how he got his name, and how he came to be living at the little settlement of Henlopen, just inside the mouth of the Delaware Bay, the story must begin as far back as 1686, when a great storm swept the Atlantic coast from end to end. During the heaviest part of the hurricane a bark went ashore on the Hen-and-Chicken Shoals, just below Cape Henlopen and at the mouth of the Delaware Bay, and Tom Chist was the only soul of all those on board the ill-fated vessel who escaped alive.

This story must first be told, because it was on account of the strange and miraculous escape that happened to him at that time that he gained the name that was given to him.

Even as late as that time of the American colonies, the little scattered settlement at Henlopen, made up of English, with a few Dutch and Swedish people, was still only a spot upon the face of the great American wilderness that spread away, with swamp and forest, no man knew how far to the westward. That wilderness was not only full of wild beasts, but of Indian savages, who every fall would come in wandering tribes to spend the winter along the shores of the fresh-water lakes below Henlopen. There for four or five months they would live upon fish and clams and wild ducks and geese, chipping their arrow-heads, and making their earthenware pots and pans under the lee of the sand-hills and pine woods below the Capes.

Sometimes on Sundays, when the Rev. Hillary Jones would be preaching in the little log church back in the woods, these half-clad red savages would come in from the cold, and sit squatting in the back part of the church, listening stolidly to the words that had no meaning for them.

But about the wreck of the bark in 1686. Such a wreck as that which then went ashore on the Hen-and-Chicken Shoals was a godsend to the poor and needy settlers in the wilderness where so few good things ever came. For the vessel went to pieces during the night, and the next morning the beach was strewn with wreckage—boxes and barrels, chests and spars, timbers and planks, a plentiful and bountiful harvest to be gathered up by the settlers as they chose, with no one to forbid or prevent them.

The name of the bark, as found painted on some of the water-barrels and sea-chests, was the *Bristol Merchant,* and she no doubt hailed from England.

As was said, the only soul who escaped alive off the wreck was Tom Chist.

A settler, a fisherman named Matt Abrahamson, and his daughter Molly, found Tom. He was washed up on the beach among the wreckage, in a great wooden box which had been securely tied around with a rope and lashed between two spars—apparently for better protection in beating through the surf. Matt Abrahamson thought he had found something of more than usual value when he came upon this chest; but when he cut the cords and broke open the box with his broadaxe, he could not have been more astonished had he beheld a salamander instead of a baby of nine or ten months old lying half smothered in the blankets that covered the bottom of the chest.

Matt Abrahamson's daughter Molly had had a baby who had died a month or so before. So when she saw the little one lying there in the bottom of the chest, she cried out in a great loud voice that the Good Man had sent her another baby in place of her own.

The rain was driving before the hurricane-storm in dim, slanting sheets, and so she wrapped up the baby in the man's coat she wore and ran off home without waiting to gather up any more of the wreckage.

It was Parson Jones who gave the foundling his name. When the news came to his ears of what Matt Abrahamson had found, he went over to the fisherman's cabin to see the child. He examined the clothes in which the baby was dressed. They were of fine linen and handsomely stitched, and the reverend gentleman opined that the foundling's parents must have been of quality. A kerchief had been wrapped around the baby's neck and under its arms and tied behind, and in the corner, marked with very fine needlework, were the initials T.C.

"What d'ye call him, Molly?" said Parson Jones. He was standing, as he spoke, with his back to the fire, warming his palms before the blaze. The pocket of the great-coat he wore bulged out with a big case-bottle of spirits which he had gathered up out of the wreck that afternoon. "What d'ye call him, Molly?"

"I'll call him Tom, after my own baby."

"That goes very well with the initial on the kerchief," said Parson Jones. "But what other name d'ye give him? Let it be something to go with the C."

"I don't know," said Molly.

"Why not call him 'Chist,' since he was born in a chist out of the sea? 'Tom Chist' — the name goes off like a flash in the pan." And so "Tom Chist" he was called and "Tom Chist" he was christened.

So much for the beginning of the history of Tom Chist. The story of Captain Kidd's treasure-box does not begin until the late spring of

1699.

That was the year that the famous pirate captain, coming up from the West Indies, sailed his sloop into the Delaware Bay, where he lay for over a month waiting for news from his friends in New York.

For he had sent word to that town asking if the coast was clear for him to return home with the rich prize he had brought from the Indian seas and the coast of Africa, and meantime he lay there in the Delaware Bay waiting for a reply. Before he left he turned the whole of Tom Chist's life topsy-turvy with something that he brought ashore.

By that time Tom Chist had grown into a strong-limbed, thick-jointed boy of fourteen or fifteen years of age. It was a miserable dog's life he lived with old Matt Abrahamson, for the old fisherman was in his cups more than half the time, and when he was so there was hardly a day passed that he did not give Tom a curse or a buffet or, as like as not, an actual beating. One would have thought that such treatment would have broken the spirit of the poor little foundling, but it had just the opposite effect upon Tom Chist, who was one of your stubborn, sturdy, stiff-willed fellows who only grow harder and more tough the more they are ill-treated. It had been a long time now since he had made any outcry or complaint at the hard usage he suffered from old Matt. At such times he would shut his teeth and bear whatever came to him, until sometimes the half-drunken old man would be driven almost mad by his stubborn silence. Maybe he would stop in the midst of the beating he was administering, and, grinding his teeth, would cry out: "Won't ye say naught? Won't ye say naught? Well, then, I'll see if I can't make ye say naught." When things had reached such a pass as this Molly would generally interfere to protect her foster-son, and then she and Tom would together fight the old man until they had wrenched the stick or the strap out of his hand. Then old Matt would chase them out-of-doors and around and around the house for maybe half an hour until his anger was cool, when he would go back again, and for a time the storm would be over.

Besides his foster-mother, Tom Chist had a very good friend in Parson Jones, who used to come over every now and then to Abrahamson's hut upon the chance of getting a half-dozen fish for breakfast. He always had a kind word or two for Tom, who during the winter evenings would go over to the good man's house to learn his letters, and to read and write and cipher a little, so that by now he was able to spell the words out of the Bible and the almanac, and knew enough to change tuppence into four ha'pennies.

This is the sort of boy Tom Chist was, and this is the sort of life he led.

In the late spring or early summer of 1699 Captain Kidd's sloop sailed into the mouth of the Delaware Bay and changed the whole fortune of his life.

And this is how you come to the story of Captain Kidd's treasure-box.

II

Old Matt Abrahamson kept the flat-bottomed boat in which he went fishing some distance down the shore, and in the neighborhood of the old wreck that had been sunk on the Shoals. This was the usual fishing-ground of the settlers, and here Old Matt's boat generally lay drawn up on the sand.

There had been a thunder-storm that afternoon, and Tom had gone down the beach to bale out the boat in readiness for the morning's fishing.

It was full moonlight now, as he was returning, and the night sky was full of floating clouds. Now and then there was a dull flash to the westward, and once a muttering growl of thunder, promising another storm to come.

All that day the pirate sloop had been lying just off the shore back of the Capes, and now Tom Chist could see the sails glimmering pallidly in the moonlight, spread for drying after the storm. He was walking up the shore homeward when he became aware that at some distance ahead of him there was a ship's boat drawn up on the little narrow beach, and a group of men clustered about it. He hurried forward with a good deal of curiosity to see who had landed, but it was not until he had come close to them that he could distinguish who and what they were. Then he knew that it must be a party who had come off the pirate sloop. They had evidently just landed, and two men were lifting out a chest from the boat. One of them was a negro, naked to the waist, and the other was a white man in his shirt-sleeves, wearing petticoat breeches, a Monterey cap upon his head, a red bandanna handkerchief around his neck, and gold ear-rings in his ears. He had a long, plaited queue hanging down his back, and a great sheath-knife dangling from his side. Another man, evidently the captain of the party, stood at a little distance as they lifted the chest out of the boat. He had a cane in one hand and a lighted lantern in the other, although the moon was shining as bright as day. He wore jack-boots and a handsome laced coat, and he had a long, drooping mustache that curled down below his chin. He wore a fine, feathered hat, and his long black hair hung down upon his shoulders.

All this Tom Chist could see in the moonlight that glinted and twinkled upon the gilt buttons of his coat.

They were so busy lifting the chest from the boat that at first they did not observe that Tom Chist had come up and was standing there. It was the white man with the long, plaited queue and the gold ear-rings that spoke to him. "Boy, what do you want here, boy?" he said, in a rough, hoarse voice. "Where d'ye come from?" And then dropping his end of the chest, and without giving Tom time to answer, he pointed off down the beach, and said, "You'd better be going about your own business, if you know what's good for you; and don't you come back, or you'll find what you don't want waiting for you."

Tom saw in a glance that the pirates were all looking at him, and then, without saying a word, he turned and walked away. The man who had spoken to him followed him threateningly for some little distance, as though to see that he had gone away as he was bidden to do. But presently he stopped, and Tom hurried on alone, until the boat and the crew and all were dropped away behind and lost in the moonlight night. Then he himself stopped also, turned, and looked back whence he had come.

There had been something very strange in the appearance of the men he had just seen, something very mysterious in their actions, and he wondered what it all meant, and what they were going to do. He stood for a little while thus looking and listening. He could see nothing, and could hear only the sound of distant talking. What were they doing on the lonely shore thus at night? Then, following a sudden impulse, he turned and cut off across the sand-hummocks, skirting around inland, but keeping pretty close to the shore, his object being to spy upon them, and to watch what they were about from the back of the low sand-hills that fronted the beach.

He had gone along some distance in his circuitous return when he became aware of the sound of voices that seemed to be drawing closer to him as he came towards the speakers. He stopped and stood listening, and instantly, as he stopped, the voices stopped also. He crouched there silently in the bright, glimmering moonlight, surrounded by the silent stretches of sand, and the stillness seemed to press upon him like a heavy hand. Then suddenly the sound of a man's voice began again, and as Tom listened he could hear some one slowly counting. "Ninety-one," the voice began, "ninety-two, ninety-three, ninety-four, ninety-five, ninety-six, ninety-seven, ninety-eight, ninety-nine, one hundred, one hundred and one"—the slow, monotonous count coming nearer and nearer to him—"one hundred and two, one hundred and three, one hundred and four," and so on in its monotonous reckoning.

Suddenly he saw three heads appear above the sand-hill, so close to him that he crouched down quickly with a keen thrill, close beside the hummock near which he stood. His first fear was that they might have seen him in the moonlight; but they had not, and his heart rose again as the counting voice went steadily on. "One hundred and twenty," it was saying—"and twenty-one, and twenty-two, and twenty-three, and twenty-four," and then he who was counting came out from behind the little sandy rise into the white and open level of shimmering brightness.

"AND TWENTY-ONE, AND TWENTY-TWO"

It was the man with the cane whom Tom had seen some time before—the captain of the party who had landed. He carried his cane under his arm now, and was holding his lantern close to something that he held in his hand, and upon which he looked narrowly as he walked with a slow and measured tread in a perfectly straight line across the sand, counting each step as he took it. "And twenty-five, and twenty-six, and twenty-seven, and twenty-eight, and twenty-nine, and thirty."

Behind him walked two other figures; one was the half-naked negro, the other the man with the plaited queue and the ear-rings, whom Tom had seen lifting the chest out of the boat. Now they were carrying the heavy box between them, laboring through the sand with shuffling tread as they bore it onward.

As he who was counting pronounced the word "thirty," the two men set the chest down on the sand with a grunt, the white man panting and blowing and wiping his sleeve across his forehead. And immediately he who counted took out a slip of paper and marked something down upon it. They stood there for a long time, during which Tom lay behind the sand-hummock watching them, and for a while the silence was uninterrupted. In the perfect stillness Tom could hear the washing of the little waves beating upon the distant beach, and once the far-away sound of a laugh from one of those who stood by the ship's boat.

One, two, three minutes passed, and then the men picked up the chest and started on again; and then again the other man began his counting. "Thirty and one, and thirty and two, and thirty and three, and thirty and four"—he walked straight across the level open, still looking intently at that which he held in his hand—"and thirty and five, and thirty and six, and thirty and seven," and so on, until the three figures disappeared in the little hollow between the two sand-hills on the opposite side of the open, and still Tom could hear the sound of the counting voice in the distance.

Just as they disappeared behind the hill there was a sudden faint flash of light; and by-and-by, as Tom lay still listening to the counting, he heard, after a long interval, a far-away muffled rumble of distant thunder. He waited for a while, and then arose and stepped to the top of the sand-hummock behind which he had been lying. He looked all about him, but there was no one else to be seen. Then he stepped down from the hummock and followed in the direction which the pirate captain and the two men carrying the chest had gone. He crept along cautiously, stopping now and then to make sure that he still heard the counting voice, and when it ceased he lay down upon the sand and waited until it began again.

Presently, so following the pirates, he saw the three figures again in the distance, and, skirting around back of a hill of sand covered with coarse sedge-grass, he came to where he overlooked a little open level space gleaming white in the moonlight.

The three had been crossing the level of sand, and were now not more than twenty-five paces from him. They had again set down the chest, upon which the white man with the long queue and the gold ear-rings had seated to rest himself, the negro standing close beside him. The moon shone as bright as day and full upon his face. It was looking directly at Tom Chist, every line as keen cut with white lights and black shadows as though it had been carved in ivory and jet. He sat perfectly motionless, and Tom drew back with a start, almost thinking he had been discovered. He lay silent, his heart beating heavily in his throat; but there was no alarm, and presently he heard the counting begin again, and when he looked once more he saw they were going away straight across the little open. A soft, sliding hillock of sand lay directly in front of them. They did not turn aside, but went straight over it, the leader helping himself up the sandy slope with his cane, still counting and still keeping his eyes fixed upon that which he held in his hand. Then they disappeared again behind the white crest on the other side.

So Tom followed them cautiously until they had gone almost half a mile inland. When next he saw them clearly it was from a little sandy rise which looked down like the crest of a bowl upon the floor of sand below. Upon this smooth, white floor the moon beat with almost dazzling brightness.

The white man who had helped to carry the chest was now kneeling, busied at some work, though what it was Tom at first could not see. He was whittling the point of a stick into a long wooden peg, and when, by-and-by, he had finished what he was about, he arose and stepped to where he who seemed to be the captain had stuck his cane upright into the ground as though to mark some particular spot. He drew the cane out of the sand, thrusting the stick down in its stead. Then he drove the long peg down with a wooden mallet which the negro handed to him. The sharp rapping of the mallet upon the top of the peg sounded loud in the perfect stillness, and Tom lay watching and wondering what it all meant.

The man, with quick-repeated blows, drove the peg farther and farther down into the sand until it showed only two or three inches above the surface. As he finished his work there was another faint flash of light, and by-and-by another smothered rumble of thunder, and Tom as he looked out towards the westward, saw the silver rim of the round and sharply outlined thundercloud rising slowly up into the sky and pushing the other and broken drifting clouds before it.

The two white men were now stooping over the peg, the negro man watching them. Then presently the man with the cane started straight away from the peg, carrying the end of a measuring-line with him, the other end of which the man with the plaited queue held against the top of the peg. When the pirate captain had reached the end of the measuring-line he marked a cross upon the sand, and then again they measured out another stretch of space.

So they measured a distance five times over, and then, from where Tom lay, he could see the man with the queue drive another peg just at the foot of a sloping rise of sand that swept up beyond into a tall white dune marked sharp and clear against the night sky behind. As soon as the man with the plaited queue had driven the second peg into the ground they began measuring again, and so, still measuring, disappeared in another direction which took them in behind the sand-dune, where Tom no longer could see what they were doing.

The negro still sat by the chest where the two had left him, and so bright was the moonlight that from where he lay Tom could see the glint of it twinkling in the whites of his eyeballs.

Presently from behind the hill there came, for the third time, the sharp rapping sound of the mallet driving still another peg, and then after a while the two pirates emerged from behind the sloping whiteness into the space of moonlight again.

They came direct to where the chest lay, and the white man and the black man lifting it once more, they walked away across the level of open sand, and so on behind the edge of the hill and out of Tom's sight.

III

Tom Chist could no longer see what the pirates were doing, neither did he dare to cross over the open space of sand that now lay between them and him. He lay there speculating as to what they were about, and meantime the storm cloud was rising higher and higher above the horizon, with louder and louder mutterings of thunder following each dull flash from out the cloudy, cavernous depths. In the silence he could hear an occasional click as of some iron implement, and he opined that the pirates were burying the chest, though just where they were at work he could neither see nor tell. Still he lay there watching and listening, and by-and-by a puff of warm air blew across the sand, and a thumping tumble of louder thunder leaped from out the belly of the storm cloud, which every minute was coming nearer and nearer. Still Tom Chist lay watching.

Suddenly, almost unexpectedly, the three figures reappeared from behind the sand-hill, the pirate captain leading the way, and the negro and white man following close behind him. They had gone about half-way across the white, sandy level between the hill and the hummock behind which Tom Chist lay, when the white man stopped and bent over as though to tie his shoe.

This brought the negro a few steps in front of his companion.

That which then followed happened so suddenly, so unexpectedly, so swiftly, that Tom Chist had hardly time to realize what it all meant before it was over. As the negro passed him the white man arose suddenly and silently erect, and Tom Chist saw the white moonlight glint upon the blade of a great dirk-knife which he now held in his hand. He took one, two silent, catlike steps behind the unsuspecting negro. Then there was a sweeping flash of the blade in the pallid light, and a blow, the thump of which Tom could distinctly hear even from where he lay stretched out upon the sand. There was an instant echoing yell from the black man, who ran stumbling forward, who stopped, who regained his footing, and then stood for an instant as though rooted to the spot.

Tom had distinctly seen the knife enter his back, and even thought that he had seen the glint of the point as it came out from the breast.

Meantime the pirate captain had stopped, and now stood with his hand resting upon his cane looking impassively on.

Then the black man started to run. The white man stood for a while glaring after him; then he too started after his victim upon the run. The black man was not very far from Tom when he staggered and fell. He tried to rise, then fell forward again, and lay at length. At that instant the first edge of the cloud cut across the moon, and there was a sudden darkness; but in the silence Tom heard the sound of another blow and a groan, and then presently a voice calling to the pirate captain that it was all over.

He saw the dim form of the captain crossing the level sand, and then, as the moon sailed out from behind the cloud, he saw the white man standing over a black figure that lay motionless upon the sand.

Then Tom Chist scrambled up and ran away, plunging down into the hollow of sand that lay in the shadows below. Over the next rise he ran, and down again into the next black hollow, and so on over the sliding, shifting ground, panting and gasping. It seemed to him that he could hear footsteps following, and in the terror that possessed him he almost expected every instant to feel the cold knife-blade slide between his own ribs in such a thrust from behind as he had seen given to the poor black man.

So he ran on like one in a nightmare. His feet grew heavy like lead, he panted and gasped, his breath came hot and dry in his throat. But still he ran and ran until at last he found himself in front of old Matt Abrahamson's cabin, gasping, panting, and sobbing for breath, his knees relaxed and his thighs trembling with weakness.

As he opened the door and dashed into the darkened cabin (for both Matt and Molly were long ago asleep in bed) there was a flash of light, and even as he slammed to the door behind him there was an instant peal of thunder, heavy as though a great weight had been dropped upon the roof of the sky, so that the doors and windows of the cabin rattled.

IV

Then Tom Chist crept to bed, trembling, shuddering, bathed in sweat, his heart beating like a trip-hammer, and his brain dizzy from that long, terror-inspired race through the soft sand in which he had striven to outstrip he knew not what pursuing horror.

For a long, long time he lay awake, trembling and chattering with nervous chills, and when he did fall asleep it was only to drop into monstrous dreams in which he once again saw ever enacted, with various grotesque variations, the tragic drama which his waking eyes had beheld the night before.

Then came the dawning of the broad, wet daylight, and before the rising of the sun Tom was up and out-of-doors to find the young day dripping with the rain of overnight.

His first act was to climb the nearest sandhill and to gaze out towards the offing where the pirate ship had been the day before.

It was no longer there.

Soon afterwards Matt Abrahamson came out of the cabin and he called to Tom to go get a bite to eat, for it was time for them to be away fishing.

All that morning the recollection of the night before hung over Tom Chist like a great cloud of boding trouble. It filled the confined area of the little boat and spread over the entire wide spaces of sky and sea that surrounded them. Not for a moment was it lifted. Even when he was hauling in his wet and dripping line with a struggling fish at the end of it a recurrent memory of what he had seen would suddenly come upon him, and he would groan in spirit at the recollection. He looked at Matt Abrahamson's leathery face, at his lantern jaws cavernously and stolidly chewing at a tobacco leaf, and it seemed monstrous to him that the old man should be so unconscious of the black cloud that wrapped them all about.

When the boat reached the shore again he leaped scrambling to the beach, and as soon as his dinner was eaten he hurried away to find the Dominie Jones.

He ran all the way from Abrahamson's hut to the Parson's house, hardly stopping once, and when he knocked at the door he was panting and sobbing for breath.

The good man was sitting on the back-kitchen door-step smoking his long pipe of tobacco out into the sunlight, while his wife within was rattling about among the pans and dishes in preparation of their supper, of which a strong, porky smell already filled the air.

Then Tom Chist told his story, panting, hurrying, tumbling one word over another in his haste, and Parson Jones listened, breaking every now and then into an ejaculation of wonder. The light in his pipe went out and the bowl turned cold.

"And I don't see why they should have killed the poor black man," said Tom, as he finished his narrative.

"Why, that is very easy enough to understand," said the good reverend man. "'Twas a treasure-box they buried!"

In his agitation Mr. Jones had risen from his seat and was now stumping up and down, puffing at his empty tobacco-pipe as though it were still alight.

"A treasure-box!" cried out Tom.

"Aye, a treasure-box! And that was why they killed the poor black man. He was the only one, d'ye see, besides they two who knew the place where 'twas hid, and now that they've killed him out of the way, there's nobody but themselves knows. The villains—Tut, tut, look at that now!" In his excitement the dominie had snapped the stem of his tobacco-pipe in two.

"Why, then," said Tom, "if that is so, 'tis indeed a wicked, bloody treasure, and fit to bring a curse upon anybody who finds it!"

"'Tis more like to bring a curse upon the soul who buried it," said Parson Jones, "and it may be a blessing to him who finds it. But tell me, Tom, do you think you could find the place again where 'twas hid?"

"I can't tell that," said Tom, "'twas all in among the sand-humps, d'ye see, and it was at night into the bargain. Maybe we could find the marks of their feet in the sand," he added.

"'Tis not likely," said the reverend gentleman, "for the storm last night would have washed all that away."

"I could find the place," said Tom, "where the boat was drawn up on the beach."

"Why, then, that's something to start from, Tom," said his friend. "If we can find that, then maybe we can find whither they went from there."

"If I was certain it was a treasure-box," cried out Tom Chist, "I would rake over every foot of sand betwixt here and Henlopen to find it."

"'Twould be like hunting for a pin in a haystack," said the Rev. Hilary Jones.

As Tom walked away home, it seemed as though a ton's weight of gloom had been rolled away from his soul. The next day he and Parson Jones were to go treasure-hunting together; it seemed to Tom as though he could hardly wait for the time to come.

V

The next afternoon Parson Jones and Tom Chist started off together upon the expedition that made Tom's fortune forever. Tom carried a spade over his shoulder and the reverend gentleman walked along beside him with his cane.

As they jogged along up the beach they talked together about the only thing they could talk about—the treasure-box. "And how big did you say 'twas?" quoth the good gentleman.

"About so long," said Tom Chist, measuring off upon the spade, "and about so wide, and this deep."

"And what if it should be full of money, Tom?" said the reverend gentleman, swinging his cane around and around in wide circles in the excitement of the thought, as he strode along briskly. "Suppose it should be full of money, what then?"

"By Moses!" said Tom Chist, hurrying to keep up with his friend, "I'd buy a ship for myself, I would, and I'd trade to Injy and to Chiny to my own boot, I would. Suppose the chist was all full of money, sir, and suppose we should find it; would there be enough in it, d'ye suppose, to buy a ship?"

"To be sure there would be enough, Tom; enough and to spare, and a good big lump over."

"And if I find it 'tis mine to keep, is it, and no mistake?"

"Why, to be sure it would be yours!" cried out the Parson, in a loud voice. "To be sure it would be yours!" He knew nothing of the law, but the doubt of the question began at once to ferment in his brain, and he strode along in silence for a while. "Whose else would it be but yours if you find it?" he burst out. "Can you tell me that?"

"If ever I have a ship of my own," said Tom Chist, "and if ever I sail to Injy in her, I'll fetch ye back the best chist of tea, sir, that ever was fetched from Cochin Chiny."

Parson Jones burst out laughing. "Thankee, Tom," he said; "and I'll thankee again when I get my chist of tea. But tell me, Tom, didst thou ever hear of the farmer girl who counted her chickens before they were hatched?"

It was thus they talked as they hurried along up the beach together, and so came to a place at last where Tom stopped short and stood looking about him. "'Twas just here," he said, "I saw the boat last night. I know 'twas here, for I mind me of that bit of wreck yonder, and that there was a tall stake drove in the sand just where yon stake stands."

Parson Jones put on his barnacles and went over to the stake towards which Tom pointed. As soon as he had looked at it carefully, he called out: "Why, Tom, this hath been just drove down into the sand. 'Tis a brand-new stake of wood, and the pirates must have set it here themselves as a mark, just as they drove the pegs you spoke about down into the sand."

Tom came over and looked at the stake. It was a stout piece of oak nearly two inches thick; it had been shaped with some care, and the top of it had been painted red. He shook the stake and tried to move it, but it had been driven or planted so deeply into the sand that he could not stir it. "Aye, sir," he said, "it must have been set here for a mark, for I'm sure 'twas not here yesterday or the day before." He stood looking about him to see if there were other signs of the pirates' presence. At some little distance there was the corner of something white sticking up out of the sand. He could see that it was a scrap of paper, and he pointed to it, calling out: "Yonder is a piece of paper, sir. I wonder if they left that behind them?"

It was a miraculous chance that placed that paper there. There was only an inch of it showing, and if it had not been for Tom's sharp eyes, it would certainly have been overlooked and passed by. The next wind-storm would have covered it up, and all that afterwards happened never would have occurred. "Look sir," he said, as he struck the sand from it, "it hath writing on it."

"Let me see it," said Parson Jones. He adjusted the spectacles a little more firmly astride of his nose as he took the paper in his hand and began conning it. "What's all this?" he said; "a whole lot of figures and nothing else." And then he read aloud, "'Mark—S.S.W. by S.' What d'ye suppose that means, Tom?"

"I don't know, sir," said Tom. "But maybe we can understand it better if you read on."

"'Tis all a great lot of figures," said Parson Jones, "without a grain of meaning in them so far as I can see, unless they be sailing directions." And then he began reading again: "'Mark—S.S.W. by S. 40, 72, 91, 130, 151, 177,

202, 232, 256, 271′—d′ye see, it must be sailing directions—′299, 335, 362, 386, 415, 446, 469, 491, 522, 544, 571, 598′—what a lot of them there be—′626, 652, 676, 695, 724, 851, 876, 905, 940, 967. Peg. S.E. by E. 269 foot. Peg. S.S.W. by S. 427 foot. Peg. Dig to the west of this six foot.′"

"What's that about a peg?" exclaimed Tom. "What's that about a peg? And then there's something about digging, too!" It was as though a sudden light began shining into his brain. He felt himself growing quickly very excited. "Read that over again, sir," he cried. "Why, sir, you remember I told you they drove a peg into the sand. And don't they say to dig close to it? Read it over again, sir—read it over again!"

"Peg?" said the good gentleman. "To be sure it was about a peg. Let's look again. Yes, here it is. 'Peg S.E. by E. 269 foot.'"

"Aye!" cried out Tom Chist again, in great excitement. "Don't you remember what I told you, sir, 269 foot? Sure that must be what I saw 'em measuring with the line." Parson Jones had now caught the flame of excitement that was blazing up so strongly in Tom's breast. He felt as though some wonderful thing was about to happen to them. "To be sure, to be sure!" he called out, in a great big voice. "And then they measured out 427 foot south-southwest by south, and then they drove another peg, and then they buried the box six foot to the west of it. Why, Tom—why, Tom Chist! if we've read this aright, thy fortune is made."

Tom Chist stood staring straight at the old gentleman's excited face, and seeing nothing but it in all the bright infinity of sunshine. Were they, indeed, about to find the treasure-chest? He felt the sun very hot upon his shoulders, and he heard the harsh, insistent jarring of a tern that hovered and circled with forked tail and sharp white wings in the sunlight just above their heads; but all the time he stood staring into the good old gentleman's face.

It was Parson Jones who first spoke. "But what do all these figures mean?" And Tom observed how the paper shook and rustled in the tremor of excitement that shook his hand. He raised the paper to the focus of his spectacles and began to read again. "'Mark 40, 72, 91—'"

"Mark?" cried out Tom, almost screaming. "Why, that must mean the stake yonder; that must be the mark." And he pointed to the oaken stick with its red tip blazing against the white shimmer of sand behind it.

"And the 40 and 72 and 91," cried the old gentleman, in a voice equally shrill—"why, that must mean the number of steps the pirate was counting when you heard him."

"To be sure that's what they mean!" cried Tom Chist. "That is it, and it can be nothing else. Oh, come, sir—come, sir; let us make haste and find it!"

"Stay! stay!" said the good gentleman, holding up his hand; and again Tom Chist noticed how it trembled and shook. His voice was steady enough, though very hoarse, but his hand shook and trembled as though with a palsy. "Stay! stay! First of all, we must follow these measurements. And 'tis a marvellous thing," he croaked, after a little pause, "how this paper ever came to be here."

"Maybe it was blown here by the storm," suggested Tom Chist.

"Like enough; like enough," said Parson Jones. "Like enough, after the wretches had buried the chest and killed the poor black man, they were so buffeted and bowsed about by the storm that it was shook out of the man's pocket, and thus blew away from him without his knowing aught of it."

"But let us find the box!" cried out Tom Chist, flaming with his excitement.

"Aye, aye," said the good man; "only stay a little, my boy, until we make sure what we're about. I've got my pocket-compass here, but we must have something to measure off the feet when we have found the peg. You run across to Tom Brooke's house and fetch that measuring-rod he used to lay out his new byre. While you're gone I'll pace off the distance marked on the paper with my pocket-compass here."

VI

Tom Chist was gone for almost an hour, though he ran nearly all the way and back, upborne as on the wings of the wind. When he returned, panting, Parson Jones was nowhere to be seen, but Tom saw his footsteps leading away inland, and he followed the scuffling marks in the smooth surface across the sand-humps and down into the hollows, and by-and-by found the good gentleman in a spot he at once knew as soon as he laid his eyes upon it.

It was the open space where the pirates had driven their first peg, and where Tom Chist had afterwards seen them kill the poor black man. Tom Chist gazed around as though expecting to see some sign of the tragedy, but the space was as smooth and as undisturbed as a floor, excepting where, midway across it, Parson Jones who was now stooping over something on the ground, had trampled it all around about.

When Tom Chist saw him, he was still bending over, scraping the sand away from something he had found.

It was the first peg!

Inside of half an hour they had found the second and third pegs, and Tom Chist stripped off his coat, and began digging like mad down into the sand, Parson Jones standing over him watching him. The sun was sloping well towards the west when the blade of Tom Chist's spade struck upon something hard.

If it had been his own heart that he had hit in the sand his breast could hardly have thrilled more sharply.

It was the treasure-box!

Parson Jones himself leaped down into the hole, and began scraping away the sand with his hands as though he had gone crazy. At last, with some difficulty, they tugged and hauled the chest up out of the sand to the surface, where it lay covered all over with the grit that clung to it.

It was securely locked and fastened with a padlock, and it took a good many blows with the blade of the spade to burst the bolt. Parson Jones himself lifted the lid.

Tom Chist leaned forward and gazed down into the open box. He would not have been surprised to have seen it filled full of yellow gold and bright jewels. It was filled half full of books and papers, and half full of canvas bags tied safely and securely around and around with cords of string.

Parson Jones lifted out one of the bags, and it jingled as he did so. It was full of money.

He cut the string, and with trembling, shaking hands handed the bag to Tom, who, in an ecstasy of wonder and dizzy with delight, poured out with swimming sight upon the coat spread on the ground a cataract of shining silver money that rang and twinkled and jingled as it fell in a shining heap upon the coarse cloth.

Parson Jones held up both hands into the air, and Tom stared at what he saw, wondering whether it was all so, and whether he was really awake. It seemed to him as though he was in a dream.

There were two-and-twenty bags in all in the chest: ten of them full of silver money, eight of them full of gold money, three of them full of gold-dust, and one small bag with jewels wrapped up in wad cotton and paper.

"'TIS ENOUGH,' CRIED OUT PARSON JONES, 'TO MAKE US BOTH RICH MEN'"

"'Tis enough," cried out Parson Jones, "to make us both rich men as long as we live."

The burning summer sun, though sloping in the sky, beat down upon them as hot as fire; but neither of them noticed it. Neither did they notice hunger nor thirst nor fatigue, but sat there as though in a trance, with the bags of money scattered on the sand around them, a great pile of money heaped upon the coat, and the open chest beside them. It was an hour of sundown before Parson Jones had begun fairly to examine the books and papers in the chest.

Of the three books, two were evidently log-books of the pirates who had been lying off the mouth of the Delaware Bay all this time. The other book was written in Spanish, and was evidently the log-book of some captured prize.

It was then, sitting there upon the sand, the good old gentleman reading in his high, cracking voice, that they first learned from the bloody records in those two books who it was who had been lying inside the Cape all this time, and that it was the famous Captain Kidd. Every now and then the reverend gentleman would stop to exclaim, "Oh, the bloody wretch!" or, "Oh, the desperate, cruel villains!" and then would go on reading again a scrap here and a scrap there.

And all the while Tom Chist sat and listened, every now and then reaching out furtively and touching the heap of money still lying upon the coat.

One might be inclined to wonder why Captain Kidd had kept those bloody records. He had probably laid them away because they so incriminated many of the great people of the colony of New York that, with the books in evidence, it would have been impossible to bring the pirate to justice without dragging a dozen or more fine gentlemen into the dock along with him. If he could have kept them in his own possession, they would doubtless have been a great weapon of defence to protect him from the gallows. Indeed, when Captain Kidd was finally brought to conviction and hung, he was not accused of his piracies, but of striking a mutinous seaman upon the head with a bucket and accidentally killing him. The authorities did not dare try him for piracy. He was really hung because he was a pirate, and we know that it was the log-books that Tom Chist brought to New York that did the business for him; he was accused and convicted of manslaughter for killing of his own ship-carpenter with a bucket.

So Parson Jones, sitting there in the slanting light, read through these terrible records of piracy, and Tom, with the pile of gold and silver money beside him, sat and listened to him.

What a spectacle, if any one had come upon them! But they were alone, with the vast arch of sky empty above them and the wide white stretch of sand a desert around them. The sun sank lower and lower, until there was only time to glance through the other papers in the chest.

They were nearly all goldsmiths' bills of exchange drawn in favor of certain of the most prominent merchants of New York. Parson Jones, as he read over the names, knew of nearly all the gentlemen by hearsay. Aye, here was this gentleman; he thought that name would be among 'em. What? Here is Mr. So-and-so. Well, if all they say is true, the villain has robbed one of his own best friends. "I wonder," he said, "why the wretch should have hidden these papers so carefully away with the other treasures, for they could do him no good?" Then, answering his own question: "Like enough because these will give him a hold over the gentlemen to whom they are drawn so that he can make a good bargain for his own neck before he gives the bills back to their owners. I tell you what it is, Tom," he continued, "it is you yourself shall go to New York and bargain for the return of these papers. 'Twill be as good as another fortune to you."

The majority of the bills were drawn in favor of one Richard Chillingsworth, Esquire. "And he is," said Parson Jones; "one of the richest men in the province of New York. You shall go to him with the news of what we have found."

"When shall I go?" said Tom Chist.

"You shall go upon the very first boat we can catch," said the Parson. He had turned, still holding the bills in his hand, and was now fingering over the pile of money that yet lay tumbled out upon the coat. "I wonder, Tom," said he, "if you could spare me a score or so of these doubloons?"

"You shall have fifty score, if you choose," said Tom, bursting with gratitude and with generosity in his newly found treasure.

"You are as fine a lad as ever I saw, Tom," said the Parson, "and I'll thank you to the last day of my life."

Tom scooped up a double handful of silver money. "Take it, sir," he said, "and you may have as much more as you want of it."

He poured it into the dish that the good man made of his hands, and the Parson made a motion as though to empty it into his pocket. Then he stopped, as though a sudden doubt had occurred to him. "I don't know that 'tis fit for me to take this pirate money, after all," he said.

"But you are welcome to it," said Tom.

Still the Parson hesitated. "Nay," he burst out, "I'll not take it; 'tis blood-money." And as he spoke he chucked the whole double handful into the now empty chest, then arose and dusted the sand from his breeches. Then, with a great deal of bustling energy, he helped to tie the bags again and put them all back into the chest.

They reburied the chest in the place whence they had taken it, and then the Parson folded the precious paper of directions, placed it carefully in his wallet, and his wallet in his pocket.

"Tom," he said, for the twentieth time, "your fortune has been made this day."

And Tom Chist, as he rattled in his breeches pocket the half-dozen doubloons he had kept out of his treasure, felt that what his friend had said was true.

As the two went back homeward across the level space of sand, Tom Chist suddenly stopped stock still and stood looking about him. "'Twas just here," he said, digging his heel down into the sand, "that they killed the poor black man."

"And here he lies buried for all time," said Parson Jones; and as he spoke he dug his cane down into the sand. Tom Chist shuddered. He would not have been surprised if the ferrule of the cane had struck something soft beneath that level surface. But it did not, nor was any sign of that tragedy ever seen again. For, whether the pirates had carried away what they had done and buried it elsewhere, or whether the storm in blowing the sand had completely levelled off and hidden all sign of that tragedy where it was enacted, certain it is that it never came to sight again—at least so far as Tom Chist and the Reverend Hillary Jones ever knew.

VII

This is the story of the treasure-box. All that remains now is to conclude the story of Tom Chist, and to tell of what came of him in the end.

He did not go back again to live with old Matt Abrahamson. Parson Jones had now taken charge of him and his fortunes, and Tom did not have to go back to the fisherman's hut.

Old Abrahamson talked a great deal about it, and would come in his cups and harangue good Parson Jones, making a vast protestation of what he would do to Tom—if he ever caught him—for running away. But Tom on all these occasions kept carefully out of his way, and nothing came of the old man's threatenings.

Tom used to go over to see his foster-mother now and then, but always when the old man was from home. And Molly Abrahamson used to warn him to keep out of her father's way. "He's in as vile a humor as ever I see, Tom," she said; "he sits sulking all day long, and 'tis my belief he'd kill ye if he caught ye."

Of course Tom said nothing, even to her, about the treasure, and he and the reverend gentleman kept the knowledge thereof to themselves. About three weeks later Parson Jones managed to get him shipped aboard of a vessel bound for New York town, and a few days later Tom Chist landed at that place. He had never been in such a town before, and he could not sufficiently wonder and marvel at the number of brick houses, at the multitude of people coming and going along the fine, hard, earthen sidewalk, at the shops and the stores where goods hung in the windows, and, most of all, the fortifications and the battery at the point, at the rows of threatening cannon, and at the scarlet-coated sentries pacing up and down the ramparts. All this was very wonderful, and so were the clustered boats riding at anchor in the harbor. It was like a new world, so different was it from the sand-hills and the sedgy levels of Henlopen.

Tom Chist took up his lodgings at a coffeehouse near to the town-hall, and thence he sent by the post-boy a letter written by Parson Jones to Master Chillingsworth. In a little while the boy returned with a message, asking Tom to come up to Mr. Chillingsworth's house that afternoon at two o'clock.

Tom went thither with a great deal of trepidation, and his heart fell away altogether when he found it a fine, grand brick house, three stories high, and with wrought-iron letters across the front.

The counting-house was in the same building; but Tom, because of Mr. Jones's letter, was conducted directly into the parlor, where the great rich man was awaiting his coming. He was sitting in a leather-covered arm-chair, smoking a pipe of tobacco, and with a bottle of fine old Madeira close to his elbow.

Tom had not had a chance to buy a new suit of clothes yet, and so he cut no very fine figure in the rough dress he had brought with him from Henlopen. Nor did Mr. Chillingsworth seem to think very highly of his appearance, for he sat looking sideways at Tom as he smoked.

"Well, my lad," he said; "and what is this great thing you have to tell me that is so mightily wonderful? I got what's-his-name—Mr. Jones's— letter, and now I am ready to hear what you have to say."

But if he thought but little of his visitor's appearance at first, he soon changed his sentiments towards him, for Tom had not spoken twenty words when Mr. Chillingsworth's whole aspect changed. He straightened himself up in his seat, laid aside his pipe, pushed away his glass of Madeira, and bade Tom take a chair. He listened without a word as Tom Chist told of the buried treasure, of how he had seen the poor negro murdered, and of how he and Parson Jones had recovered the chest again. Only once did Mr. Chillingsworth interrupt the narrative. "And to think," he cried, "that the villain this very day walks about New York town as though he were an honest man, ruffling it with the best of us! But if we can only get hold of these log-books you speak of. Go on; tell me more of this."

When Tom Chist's narrative was ended, Mr. Chillingsworth's bearing was as different as daylight is from dark. He asked a thousand questions, all in the most polite and gracious tone imaginable, and not only urged a glass of his fine old Madeira upon Tom, but asked him to stay to supper. There was nobody to be there, he said, but his wife and daughter.

Tom, all in a panic at the very thought of the two ladies, sturdily refused to stay even for the dish of tea Mr. Chillingsworth offered him.

He did not know that he was destined to stay there as long as he should live.

"And now," said Mr. Chillingsworth, "tell me about yourself."

"I have nothing to tell, your honor," said Tom, "except that I was washed up out of the sea."

"Washed up out of the sea!" exclaimed Mr. Chillingsworth. "Why, how was that? Come, begin at the beginning, and tell me all."

Thereupon Tom Chist did as he was bidden, beginning at the very beginning and telling everything just as Molly Abrahamson had often told it to him. As he continued, Mr. Chillingsworth's interest changed into an appearance of stronger and stronger excitement. Suddenly he jumped up out of his chair and began to walk up and down the room.

"Stop! stop!" he cried out at last, in the midst of something Tom was saying. "Stop! stop! Tell me; do you know the name of the vessel that was wrecked, and from which you were washed ashore?"

"I've heard it said," said Tom Chist, "'twas the *Bristol Merchant*."

"I knew it! I knew it!" exclaimed the great man, in a loud voice, flinging his hands up into the air. "I felt it was so the moment you began the story. But tell me this, was there nothing found with you with a mark or a name upon it?"

"There was a kerchief," said Tom, "marked with a T and a C."

"Theodosia Chillingsworth!" cried out the merchant. "I knew it! I knew it! Heavens! to think of anything so wonderful happening as this! Boy! boy! dost thou know who thou art? Thou art my own brother's son. His name was Oliver Chillingsworth, and he was my partner in business, and thou art his son." Then he ran out into the entryway, shouting and calling for his wife and daughter to come.

So Tom Chist—or Thomas Chillingsworth, as he now was to be called— did stay to supper, after all.

This is the story, and I hope you may like it. For Tom Chist became rich and great, as was to be supposed, and he married his pretty cousin Theodosia (who had been named for his own mother, drowned in the *Bristol Merchant*).

He did not forget his friends, but had Parson Jones brought to New York to live.

As to Molly and Matt Abrahamson, they both enjoyed a pension of ten pounds a year for as long as they lived; for now that all was well with him, Tom bore no grudge against the old fisherman for all the drubbings he had suffered.

The treasure-box was brought on to New York, and if Tom Chist did not get all the money there was in it (as Parson Jones had opined he would) he got at least a good big lump of it. And it is my belief that those log-books did more to get Captain Kidd arrested in Boston town and hanged in London than anything else that was brought up against him.

III
THE GHOST OF CAPTAIN BRAND

Being a Narrative of Certain Extraordinary Adventures that Befell Barnaby True, Esquire, of the Town of New York, in the Year 1753.

I

It is not so easy to tell why discredit should be cast upon a man because of something his grandfather may have done amiss, but the world, which is never over-nice in its discrimination as to where to lay the blame, is often pleased to make the innocent suffer instead of the guilty.

Barnaby True was a good, honest boy, as boys go, but yet was he not ever allowed altogether to forget that his grandfather had been that very famous pirate, Captain William Brand, who, after so many marvellous adventures (if one may believe the catchpenny stories and ballads that were writ about him), was murdered in Jamaica by Captain John Malyoe, the commander of his own consort, the *Adventure* galley.

It hath never been denied, that ever I heard, that up to the time of Captain Brand's being commissioned against the South Sea pirates, he had always been esteemed as honest, reputable a sea-captain as could be. When he started out upon that adventure it was with a ship, the *Royal Sovereign*, fitted out by some of the most decent merchants of New York. Governor Van Dam himself had subscribed to the adventure, and himself had signed Captain Brand's commission. So, if the unfortunate man went astray, he must have had great temptation to do so; many others behaving no better when the opportunity offered in these far-away seas, when so many rich purchases might very easily be taken and no one the wiser.

To be sure those stories and ballads made our captain to be a most wicked, profane wretch; and if he were, why God knows he suffered and paid for it, for he laid his bones in Jamaica, and never saw his home or his wife or his daughter after he had sailed away on the *Royal Sovereign* on that long, misfortunate voyage, leaving his family behind him in New York to the care of strangers.

At the time when Captain Brand so met his fate in Port Royal Harbor he had increased his flotilla to two vessels—the *Royal Sovereign* (which was the vessel that had been fitted out for him in New York, a fine brigantine and a good sailer), and the *Adventure* galley, which he had captured somewhere in the South Seas. This latter vessel he placed in command of a certain John Malyoe whom he had picked up no one knows where—a young man of very good family in England, who had turned red-handed pirate. This man, who took no more thought of a human life than he would of a broom straw, was he who afterwards murdered Captain Brand, as you shall presently hear.

With these two vessels, the *Royal Sovereign* and the *Adventure*, Captain Brand and Captain Malyoe swept the Mozambique Channel as clear as a boatswain's whistle, and after three years of piracy, having gained a great booty of gold and silver and pearls, sailed straight for the Americas, making first the island of Jamaica and the harbor of Port Royal, where they dropped anchor to wait for news from home.

But by this time the authorities had been so stirred up against our pirates that it became necessary for them to hide their booty until such time as they might make their peace with the Admiralty Courts at home. So one night Captain Brand and Captain Malyoe, with two others of the pirates, went ashore with two great chests of treasure, which they buried somewhere on the banks of the Cobra River near the place where the old Spanish fort had stood.

What happened after the treasure was thus buried no one may tell. 'Twas said that Captain Brand and Captain Malyoe fell a-quarrelling and that the upshot of the matter was that Captain Malyoe shot Captain Brand through the head, and that the pirate who was with him served Captain Brand's companion after the same fashion with a pistol bullet through the body.

After that the two murderers returned to their vessel, the *Adventure* galley, and sailed away, carrying the bloody secret of the buried treasure with them.

But this double murder of Captain Brand and his companion happened, you are to understand, some twenty years before the time of this story, and while our hero was but one year old. So now to our present history.

It is a great pity that any one should have a grandfather who ended his days in such a sort as this; but it was no fault of Barnaby True's, nor could he have done anything to prevent it, seeing he was not even born into the world at the time that his grandfather turned pirate, and that he was only one year old when Captain Brand so met his death on the Cobra River. Nevertheless, the boys with whom he went to school never tired of calling him "Pirate," and would sometimes sing for his benefit that famous catchpenny ballad beginning thus:

> "Oh! my name was Captain Brand,
> A-sailing,
> And a-sailing;
> Oh! my name was Captain Brand,
> A-sailing free.
> Oh! my name was Captain Brand,
> And I sinned by sea and land,
> For I broke God's just command,
> A-sailing free."

'Twas a vile thing to sing at the grandson of so unfortunate a man, and oftentimes Barnaby True would double up his little fists and would fight his tormentors at great odds, and would sometimes go back home with a bloody nose or a bruised eye to have his poor mother cry over him and grieve for him.

Not that his days were all of teasing and torment, either; for if his comrades did sometimes treat him so, why then there were other times when he and they were as great friends as could be, and used to go a-swimming together in the most amicable fashion where there was a bit of sandy strand below the little bluff along the East River above Fort George.

There was a clump of wide beech-trees at that place, with a fine shade and a place to lay their clothes while they swam about, splashing with their naked white bodies in the water. At these times Master Barnaby would bawl as lustily and laugh as loud as though his grandfather had been the most honest ship-chandler in the town, instead of a bloody-handed pirate who had been murdered in his sins.

Ah! It is a fine thing to look back to the days when one was a boy! Barnaby may remember how, often, when he and his companions were paddling so in the water, the soldiers off duty would come up from the fort and would maybe join them in the water, others, perhaps, standing in their red coats on the shore, looking on and smoking their pipes of tobacco.

Then there were other times when maybe the very next day after our hero had fought with great valor with his fellows he would go a-rambling with them up the Bouwerie Road with the utmost friendliness; perhaps to help them steal cherries from some old Dutch farmer, forgetting in such an adventure what a thief his own grandfather had been.

But to resume our story.

When Barnaby True was between sixteen and seventeen years old he was taken into employment in the counting-house of his stepfather, Mr. Roger Hartright, the well-known West Indian merchant, a most respectable man and one of the kindest and best of friends that anybody could have in the world.

This good gentleman had courted the favor of Barnaby's mother for a long time before he had married her. Indeed, he had so courted her before she had ever thought of marrying Jonathan True. But he not venturing to ask her in marriage, and she being a brisk, handsome woman, she chose the man who spoke out his mind, and so left the silent lover out in the cold. But so soon as she was a widow and free again, Mr. Hartright resumed his wooing, and so used to come down every Tuesday and Friday evening to sit and talk with her. Among Barnaby True's earliest memories was a recollection of the good, kind gentleman sitting in old Captain Brand's double-nailed arm-chair, the sunlight shining across his knees, over which he had spread a great red silk handkerchief, while he sipped a dish of tea with a dash of rum in it. He kept up this habit of visiting the Widow True for a long time before he could fetch himself to the point of asking anything more particular of her, and so Barnaby was nigh fourteen years old before Mr. Hartright married her, and so became our hero's dear and honored foster-father.

It was the kindness of this good man that not only found a place for Barnaby in the counting-house, but advanced him so fast that, against our hero was twenty-one years old, he had made four voyages as supercargo to the West Indies in Mr. Hartright's ship, the *Belle Helen*, and soon after he was twenty-one undertook a fifth.

Nor was it in any such subordinate position as mere supercargo that he sailed upon these adventures, but rather as the confidential agent of Mr. Hartright, who, having no likelihood of children of his own, was jealous to advance our hero to a position of trust and responsibility in the counting-house, and so would have him know all the particulars of the business and become more intimately acquainted with the correspondents and agents throughout those parts of the West Indies where the affairs of the house were most active. He would give to Barnaby the best sort of letters of introduction, so that the correspondents of Mr. Hartright throughout those parts, seeing how that gentleman had adopted our hero's interests as his own, were always at considerable pains to be very polite and obliging in showing every attention to him.

Especially among these gentlemen throughout the West Indies may be mentioned Mr. Ambrose Greenfield, a merchant of excellent standing who lived at Kingston, Jamaica. This gentleman was very particular to do all that he could to make our hero's stay in these parts as agreeable and pleasant to him as might be. Mr. Greenfield is here spoken of with a greater degree of particularity than others who might as well be remarked upon, because, as the reader shall presently discover for himself, it was through the offices of this good friend that our hero first became acquainted, not only with that lady who afterwards figured with such conspicuousness in his affairs, but also with a man who, though graced with a title, was perhaps the greatest villain who ever escaped a just fate upon the gallows.

So much for the history of Barnaby True up to the beginning of this story, without which you shall hardly be able to understand the purport of those most extraordinary adventures that afterwards befell him, nor the logic of their consequence after they had occurred.

II

Upon the occasion of our hero's fifth voyage into the West Indies he made a stay of some six or eight weeks at Kingston, in the island of Jamaica, and it was at that time that the first of those extraordinary adventures befell him, concerning which this narrative has to relate.

It was Barnaby's habit, when staying at Kingston, to take lodging with a very decent, respectable widow, by name Mrs. Anne Bolles, who, with three extremely agreeable and pleasant daughters, kept a very clean and well-served house for the accommodation of strangers visiting that island.

One morning as he sat sipping his coffee, clad only in loose cotton drawers and a jacket of the same material, and with slippers upon his feet (as is the custom in that country, where every one endeavors to keep as cool as may be), Miss Eliza, the youngest of the three daughters—a brisk, handsome miss of sixteen or seventeen—came tripping into the room and handed him a sealed letter, which she declared a stranger had just left at the door, departing incontinently so soon as he had eased himself of that commission. You may conceive of Barnaby's astonishment when he opened the note and read the remarkable words that here follow:

"*Mr. Barnaby True.*

"Sir,—Though you don't know me, I know you, and I tell you this: if you will be at Pratt's Ordinary on Friday next at eight o'clock in the evening, and will accompany the man who shall say to you, '*The Royal Sovereign is come in*' you shall learn of something the most to your advantage that ever befell you. Sir, keep this note and give it to him who shall address those words to you, so to certify that you are the man he seeks. Sir, this is the most important thing that can concern you, so you will please say nothing to nobody about it."

Such was the wording of the note which was writ in as cramped and villanous handwriting as our hero ever beheld, and which, excepting his own name, was without address, and which possessed no superscription whatever.

The first emotion that stirred Barnaby True was one of extreme and profound astonishment; the second thought that came into his mind was that maybe some witty fellow—of whom he knew a good many in that place, and wild, mad rakes they were as ever the world beheld—was attempting to play off a smart, witty jest upon him. Indeed, Miss Eliza Bolles, who was of a lively, mischievous temper, was not herself above playing such a prank should the occasion offer. With this thought in his mind Barnaby inquired of her with a good deal of particularity concerning the appearance and condition of the man who had left the note, to all of which Miss replied with so straight a face and so candid an air that he could no longer suspect her of being concerned in any trick against him, and so eased his mind of any such suspicion. The bearer of the note, she informed him, was a tall, lean man, with a red neckerchief tied around his neck and with copper buckles to his shoes, and he had the appearance of a sailor-man, having a great queue of red hair hanging down his back. But, Lord! what was such a description as that in a busy seaport town full of scores of men to fit such a likeness? Accordingly, our hero put the note away into his wallet, determining to show it to his good friend Mr. Greenfield that evening, and to ask his advice upon it.

This he did, and that gentleman's opinion was the same as his: to wit, that some wag was minded to play off a hoax upon him, and that the matter of the letter was all nothing but smoke.

III

Nevertheless, though Barnaby was thus confirmed in his opinion as to the nature of the communication he had received, he yet determined in his own mind that he would see the business through to the end and so be at Pratt's Ordinary, as the note demanded, upon the day and at the time appointed therein.

Pratt's Ordinary was at that time a very fine and famous place of its sort, with good tobacco and the best rum in the West Indies, and had a garden behind it that, sloping down to the harbor front, was planted pretty thick with palms and ferns, grouped into clusters with flowers and plants. Here were a number of tables, some in little grottos, like our Vauxhall in New York, with red and blue and white paper lanterns hung among the foliage. Thither gentlemen and ladies used sometimes to go of an evening to sit and drink lime-juice and sugar and water (and sometimes a taste of something stronger), and to look out across the water at the shipping and so to enjoy the cool of the day.

Thither, accordingly, our hero went a little before the time appointed in the note, and, passing directly through the Ordinary and to the garden beyond, chose a table at the lower end and close to the water's edge, where he could not readily be seen by any one coming into the place, and yet where he could easily view whoever should approach. Then, ordering some rum and water and a pipe of tobacco, he composed himself to watch for the arrival of those witty fellows whom he suspected would presently come thither to see the end of their prank and to enjoy his confusion.

The spot was pleasant enough, for the land breeze, blowing strong and cool, set the leaves of the palm-tree above his head to rattling and clattering continually against the darkness of the sky, where, the moon then being half full, they shone every now and then like blades of steel. The waves, also, were splashing up against the little landing-place at the foot of the garden, sounding mightily pleasant in the dusk of the evening, and sparkling all over the harbor where the moon caught the edges of the water. A great many vessels were lying at anchor in their ridings, with the dark, prodigious form of a man-of-war looming up above them in the moonlight.

There our hero sat for the best part of an hour, smoking his pipe of tobacco and sipping his rum and water, yet seeing nothing of those whom he suspected might presently come thither to laugh at him.

It was not far from half after the hour when a row-boat came suddenly out of the night and pulled up to the landing-place at the foot of the garden, and three or four men came ashore in the darkness. They landed very silently and walked up the garden pathway without saying a word, and, sitting down at an adjacent table, ordered rum and water and began drinking among themselves, speaking every now and then a word or two in a tongue that Barnaby did not well understand, but which, from certain phrases they let fall, he suspected to be Portuguese. Our hero paid no great attention to them, till by-and-by he became aware that they had fallen to whispering together and were regarding him very curiously. He felt himself growing very uneasy under this observation, which every moment grew more and more particular, and he was just beginning to suspect that this interest concerning himself might have somewhat more to do with him than mere idle curiosity, when one of the men, who was plainly the captain of the party, suddenly says to him, "How now, messmate; won't you come and have a drop of drink with us?"

At this address Barnaby instantly began to be aware that the affair he had come upon was indeed no jest, as he had supposed it to be, but that he had walked into what promised to be a very pretty adventure. Nevertheless, not wishing to be too hasty in his conclusions, he answered very civilly that he had drunk enough already, and that more would only heat his blood.

"Well," says the stranger, "I may be mistook, but I believe you are Mr. Barnaby True."

"You are right, sir, and that is my name," acknowledged Barnaby. "But still I cannot guess how that may concern you, nor why it should be a reason for my drinking with you." "That I will presently tell you," says the stranger, very composedly. "Your name concerns me because I was sent here to tell Mr. Barnaby True that '*the Royal Sovereign is come in.*'"

To be sure our hero's heart jumped into his throat at those words. His pulse began beating at a tremendous rate, for here, indeed, was an adventure suddenly opening to him such as a man may read about in a book, but which he may hardly expect to befall him in the real happenings of his life. Had he been a wiser and an older man he might have declined the whole business, instead of walking blindly into that of which he could see neither the beginning nor the ending; but being barely one-and-twenty years of age, and possessing a sanguine temper and an adventurous disposition that would have carried him into almost anything that possessed a smack of uncertainty or danger, he contrived to say, in a pretty easy tone (though God knows how it was put on for the occasion):

"Well, if that be so, and if the *Royal Sovereign* is indeed come in, why, then, I'll join you, since you are so kind as to ask me." Therewith he arose and went across to the other table, carrying his pipe with him, and sat down and began smoking, with all the appearance of ease he could command upon the occasion.

At this the other burst out a-laughing. "Indeed," says he, "you are a cool blade, and a chip of the old block. But harkee, young gentleman," and here he fell serious again. "This is too weighty a business to chance any mistake in a name. I believe that you are, as you say, Mr. Barnaby True; but, nevertheless, to make perfectly sure, I must ask you first to show me a note that you have about you and which you are instructed to show to me."

"Very well," said Barnaby; "I have it here safe and sound, and you shall see it." And thereupon and without more ado he drew out his wallet, opened it, and handed the other the mysterious note which he had kept carefully by him ever since he had received it. His interlocutor took the paper, and drawing to him the candle, burning there for the convenience of those who would smoke tobacco, began immediately reading it.

This gave Barnaby True a moment or two to look at him. He was a tall, lean man with a red handkerchief tied around his neck, with a queue of red hair hanging down his back, and with copper buckles on his shoes, so that Barnaby True could not but suspect that he was the very same man who had given the note to Miss Eliza Bolles at the door of his lodging-house.

"'Tis all right and straight and as it should be," the other said, after he had so examined the note. "And now that the paper is read" (suiting his action to his words), "I'll just burn it for safety's sake."

And so he did, twisting it up and setting it to the flame of the candle. "And now," he said, continuing his address, "I'll tell you what I am here for.

I was sent to ask if you're man enough to take your life in your hands and to go with me in that boat down yonder at the foot of the garden. Say 'Yes,' and we'll start away without wasting more time, for the devil is ashore here at Jamaica—though you don't know what that means—and if he gets ahead of us, why then we may whistle for what we are after, for all the good 'twill do us. Say 'No,' and I go away, and I promise you you shall never be troubled more in this sort of a way. So now speak up plain, young gentleman, and tell us what is your wish in this business, and whether you will adventure any further or no."

If our hero hesitated it was not for long, and when he spoke up it was with a voice as steady as could be.

"To be sure I'm man enough to go with you," says he; "and if you mean me any harm I can look out for myself; and if I can't, then here is something can look out for me." And therewith he lifted up the flap of his pocket and showed the butt of a pistol he had fetched with him when he had set out from his lodging-house that evening.

At this the other burst out a-laughing for a second time. "Come," says he; "you are indeed of right mettle, and I like your spirit. All the same, no one in all the world means you less ill than I, and so, if you have to use that barker, 'twill not be upon us who are your friends, but only upon one who is more wicked than the devil himself. So now if you are prepared and have made up your mind and are determined to see this affair through to the end, 'tis time for us to be away." Whereupon, our hero indicating his acquiescence, his interlocutor and the others (who had not spoken a single word for all this time), rose together from the table, and the stranger having paid the scores of all, they went down together to the boat that lay plainly awaiting their coming at the bottom of the garden.

Thus coming to it, our hero could see that it was a large yawl-boat manned by half a score of black men for rowers, and that there were two lanterns in the stern-sheets, and three or four shovels.

The man who had conducted the conversation with Barnaby True for all this time, and who was, as has been said, plainly the captain of the expedition, stepped immediately down into the boat; our hero followed, and the others followed after him; and instantly they were seated the boat shoved off and the black men began pulling straight out into the harbor, and so, at some distance away, around under the stern of the man-of-war.

Not a word was spoken after they had thus left the shore, and they might all have been so many spirits for the silence of the party. Barnaby True was too full of his own thoughts to talk (and serious enough thoughts they were by this time, with crimps to trepan a man at every turn, and press-gangs to carry him off so that he might never be heard of again). As for the others, they did not seem to choose to say anything now that they had been fairly embarked upon their enterprise, and so the crew pulled away for the best part of an hour, the leader of the expedition directing the course of the boat straight across the harbor, as though towards the mouth of the Cobra River. Indeed, this was their destination, as Barnaby could after a while see for himself, by the low point of land with a great, long row of cocoanut-palms growing upon it (the appearance of which he knew very well), which by-and-by began to loom up from the dimness of the moonlight. As they approached the river they found the tide was running very violently, so that it gurgled and rippled alongside the boat as the crew of black men pulled strongly against it. Thus rowing slowly against the stream they came around what appeared to be either a point of land or an islet covered with a thick growth of mangrove-trees; though still no one spoke a single word as to their destination, or what was the business they had in hand.

The night, now that they had come close to the shore, appeared to be full of the noises of running tide-water, and the air was heavy with the smell of mud and marsh. And over all was the whiteness of the moonlight, with a few stars pricking out here and there in the sky; and everything was so strange and mysterious and so different from anything that he had experienced before that Barnaby could not divest himself of the feeling that it was all a dream from which at any moment he might awaken. As for the town and the Ordinary he had quitted such a short time before, so different were they from this present experience, it was as though they might have concerned another life than that which he was then enjoying.

Meantime, the rowers bending to the oars, the boat drew slowly around into the open water once more. As it did so the leader of the expedition of a sudden called out in a loud, commanding voice, whereat the black men instantly ceased rowing and lay on their oars, the boat drifting onward into the night.

At the same moment of time our hero became aware of another boat coming down the river towards where they lay. This other boat, approaching thus strangely through the darkness, was full of men, some of them armed; for even in the distance Barnaby could not but observe that the light of the moon glimmered now and then as upon the barrels of muskets or pistols. This threw him into a good deal of disquietude of mind, for whether they or this boat were friends or enemies, or as to what was to happen next, he was altogether in the dark.

Upon this point, however, he was not left very long in doubt, for the oarsmen of the approaching boat continuing to row steadily onward till they had come pretty close to Barnaby and his companions, a man who sat in the stern suddenly stood up, and as they passed by shook a cane at Barnaby's companion with a most threatening and angry gesture. At the same moment, the moonlight shining full upon him, Barnaby could see him as plain as daylight—a large, stout gentleman with a round red face, and clad in a fine, laced coat of red cloth. In the stern of the boat near by him was a box or chest about the bigness of a middle-sized travelling-trunk, but covered all over with cakes of sand and dirt. In the act of passing, the gentleman, still standing, pointed at this chest with his cane—an elegant gold-headed staff—and roared out in a loud voice: "Are you come after this, Abram Dowling? Then come and take it." And thereat, as he sat down again, burst out a-laughing as though what he had said was the wittiest jest conceivable.

Either because he respected the armed men in the other boat, or else for some reason best known to himself, the Captain of our hero's expedition did not immediately reply, but sat as still as any stone. But at last, the other boat having drifted pretty far away, he suddenly found words to shout out after it: "Very well, Jack Malyoe! Very well, Jack Malyoe! You've got the better of us once more. But next time is the third, and then it'll be our turn, even if William Brand must come back from the grave to settle with you himself."

But to this my fine gentleman in t'other boat made no reply except to burst out once more into a great fit of laughter.

There was, however, still another man in the stern of the enemy's boat—a villanous, lean man with lantern-jaws, and the top of his head as bald as an apple. He held in his hand a great pistol, which he flourished about him, crying out to the gentleman beside him, "Do but give me the word, your honor, and I'll put another bullet through the son of a sea cook." But the other forbade him, and therewith the boat presently melted away into the darkness of the night and was gone.

This happened all in a few seconds, so that before our hero understood what was passing he found the boat in which he still sat drifting silently in the moonlight (for no one spoke for awhile) and the oars of the other boat sounding farther and farther away into the distance.

By-and-by says one of those in Barnaby's boat, in Spanish, "Where shall you go now?"

At this the leader of the expedition appeared suddenly to come back to himself and to find his tongue again. "Go?" he roared out. "Go to the devil!

Go? Go where you choose! Go? Go back again—that's where well go!" And therewith he fell a-cursing and swearing, frothing at the lips as though he had gone clean crazy, while the black men, bending once more to their oars, rowed back again across the harbor as fast as ever they could lay oars to the water.

They put Barnaby True ashore below the old custom-house, but so bewildered and amazed by all that had happened, and by what he had seen, and by the names he had heard spoken, that he was only half conscious of the familiar things among which he suddenly found himself transported. The moonlight and the night appeared to have taken upon them a new and singular aspect, and he walked up the street towards his lodging like one drunk or in a dream. For you must remember that "John Malyoe" was the captain of the *Adventure* galley—he who had shot Barnaby's own grandfather—and "Abram Dowling," I must tell you, had been the gunner of the *Royal Sovereign*—he who had been shot at the same time that Captain Brand met his tragical end. And yet these names he had heard spoken—the one from one boat, and the other from the other, so that he could not but wonder what sort of beings they were among whom he had fallen.

As to that box covered all over with mud, he could only offer a conjecture as to what it contained and as to what the finding of it signified.

But of this our hero said nothing to any one, nor did he tell any one what he suspected, for, though he was so young in years, he possessed a continent disposition inherited from his father (who had been one of ten children born to a poor but worthy Presbyterian minister of Bluefield, Connecticut), so it was that not even to his good friend Mr. Greenfield did Barnaby say a word as to what had happened to him, going about his business the next day as though nothing of moment had occurred.

But he was not destined yet to be done with those beings among whom he had fallen that night; for that which he supposed to be the ending of the whole affair was only the beginning of further adventures that were soon to befall him.

IV

Mr. Greenfield lived in a fine brick house just outside of the town, on the Mona Road. His family consisted of a wife and two daughters— handsome, lively young ladies with very fine, bright teeth that shone whenever they laughed, and with a-plenty to say for themselves. To this pleasant house Barnaby True was often asked to a family dinner, after which he and his good kind host would maybe sit upon the veranda, looking out towards the mountain, smoking their cigarros while the young ladies laughed and talked, or played upon the guitar and sang.

A day or two before the *Belle Helen* sailed from Kingston, upon her return voyage to New York, Mr. Greenfield stopped Barnaby True as he was passing through the office, and begged him to come to dinner that night. (For within the tropics, you are to know, they breakfast at eleven o'clock and take dinner in the cool of the evening, because of the heat, and not at mid-day, as we do in more temperate latitudes). "I would," says Mr. Greenfield, "have you meet Sir John Malyoe and Miss Marjorie, who are to be your chief passengers for New York, and for whom the state cabin and the two state-rooms are to be fitted as here ordered"—showing a letter—"for Sir John hath arranged," says Mr. Greenfield, "for the Captain's own state-room."

Then, not being aware of Barnaby True's history, nor that Captain Brand was his grandfather, the good gentleman—calling Sir John "Jack" Malyoe—goes on to tell our hero what a famous pirate he had been, and how it was he who had shot Captain Brand over t'other side of the harbor twenty years before. "Yes," says he, "'tis the same Jack Malyoe, though grown into repute and importance now, as who would not who hath had the good-fortune to fall heir to a baronetcy and a landed estate?"

And so it befell that same night that Barnaby True once again beheld the man who had murdered his own grandfather, meeting him this time face to face.

That time in the harbor he had seen Sir John Malyoe at a distance and in the darkness; now that he beheld him closer, it seemed to him that he had never seen a countenance more distasteful to him in all his life. Not that the man was altogether ugly, for he had a good enough nose and a fine double chin; but his eyes stood out from his face and were red and watery, and he winked them continually, as though they were always a-smarting. His lips were thick and purple-red, and his cheeks mottled here and there with little clots of veins.

When he spoke, his voice rattled in his throat to such a degree that it made one wish to clear one's own throat to listen to him. So, what with a pair of fat, white hands, and that hoarse voice, and his swollen face, and his thick lips a-sticking out, it appeared to Barnaby True he had never beheld a countenance that pleased him so little.

But if Sir John Malyoe suited our hero's taste so ill, the granddaughter was in the same degree pleasing to him. She had a thin, fair skin, red lips, and yellow hair—though it was then powdered pretty white for the occasion—and the bluest eyes that ever he beheld in all of his life. A sweet, timid creature, who appeared not to dare so much as to speak a word for herself without looking to that great beast, her grandfather, for leave to do so, for she would shrink and shudder whenever he would speak of a sudden to her or direct a glance upon her. When she did pluck up sufficient courage to say anything, it was in so low a voice that Barnaby was obliged to bend his head to hear her; and when she smiled she would as like as not catch herself short and look up as though to see if she did amiss to be cheerful.

As for Sir John, he sat at dinner and gobbled and ate and drank, smacking his lips all the while, but with hardly a word of civility either to Mr. Greenfield or to Mrs. Greenfield or to Barnaby True; but wearing all the while a dull, sullen air, as though he would say, "Your damned victuals and drink are no better than they should be, but, such as they are, I must eat 'em or eat nothing."

It was only after dinner was over and the young lady and the two misses off in a corner together that Barnaby heard her talk with any degree of ease. Then, to be sure, her tongue became loose enough, and she prattled away at a great rate; though hardly above her breath. Then of a sudden her grand-father called out, in his hoarse, rattling voice, that it was time to go, upon which she stopped short in what she was saying and jumped up from her chair, looking as frightened as though he were going to strike her with that gold-headed cane of his that he always carried with him.

Barnaby True and Mr. Greenfield both went out to see the two into their coach, where Sir John's man stood holding the lantern. And who should he be, to be sure, but that same lean villain with bald head who had offered to shoot the Captain of Barnaby's expedition out on the harbor that night! For one of the circles of light shining up into his face, Barnaby True knew him the moment he clapped eyes upon him. Though he could not have recognized our hero, he grinned at him in the most impudent, familiar fashion, and never so much as touched his hat either to him or to Mr. Greenfield; but as soon as his master and his young mistress had entered the coach, banged to the door and scrambled up on the seat alongside the driver, and so away without a word, but with another impudent grin, this time favoring both Barnaby and the old gentleman.

Such were Sir John Malyoe and his man, and the ill opinion our hero conceived of them was only confirmed by further observation.

The next day Sir John Malyoe's travelling-cases began to come aboard the *Belle Helen*, and in the afternoon that same lean, villanous man-servant comes skipping across the gangplank as nimble as a goat, with two black men behind him lugging a great sea-chest. "What!" he cries out, "and so you is the supercargo, is you? Why, to be sure, I thought you was more account when I saw you last night a-sitting talking with his honor like his equal. Well, no matter," says he, "'tis something to have a brisk, genteel young fellow for a supercargo. So come, my hearty, lend a hand and help me set his honor's cabin to rights."

What a speech was this to endure from such a fellow! What with our hero's distaste for the villain, and what with such odious familiarity, you may guess into what temper so impudent an address must have cast him. Says he, "You'll find the steward in yonder, and he'll show you the cabin Sir John is to occupy." Therewith he turned and walked away with prodigious dignity, leaving the other standing where he was.

As he went below to his own state-room he could not but see, out of the tail of his eye, that the fellow was still standing where he had left him, regarding him with a most evil, malevolent countenance, so that he had the satisfaction of knowing that he had an enemy aboard for that voyage who was not very likely to forgive or forget what he must regard as so mortifying a slight as that which Barnaby had put upon him.

The next day Sir John Malyoe himself came aboard, accompanied by his granddaughter, and followed by his man, and he followed again by four black men, who carried among them two trunks, not large in size, but vastly heavy in weight. Towards these two trunks Sir John and his follower devoted the utmost solicitude and care to see that they were properly carried into the cabin he was to occupy. Barnaby True was standing in the saloon as they passed close by him; but though Sir John looked hard at him and straight in the face, he never so much as spoke a single word to our hero, or showed by a look or a sign that he had ever met him before. At this the serving-man, who saw it all with eyes as quick as a cat's, fell to grinning and chuckling to see Barnaby in his turn so slighted.

The young lady, who also saw it, blushed as red as fire, and thereupon delivered a courtesy to poor Barnaby, with a most sweet and gracious affability.

There were, besides Sir John and the young lady, but two other passengers who upon this occasion took the voyage to New York: the Reverend Simon Styles, master of a flourishing academy at Spanish Town, and his wife. This was a good, worthy couple of an extremely quiet disposition, saying little or nothing, but contented to sit in the great cabin by the hour together reading in some book or other. So, what with the retiring humor of the worthy pair, and what with Sir John Malyoe's fancy for staying all the time shut up in his own cabin with those two trunks he held so precious, it fell upon Barnaby True in great part to show that attention to the young lady that the circumstances demanded. This he did with a great deal of satisfaction to himself—as any one may suppose who considers a spirited young man of one-and-twenty years of age and a sweet and beautiful young miss of seventeen or eighteen thrown thus together day after day for above two weeks.

Accordingly, the weather being very fair and the ship driving freely along before a fine breeze, and they having no other occupation than to sit talking together all day, gazing at the blue sea and the bright sky overhead, it is not difficult to conceive of what was to befall.

But oh, those days when a man is young and, whether wisely or no, fallen into such a transport of passion as poor Barnaby True suffered at that time! How often during that voyage did our hero lie awake in his berth at night, tossing this way and that without finding any refreshment of sleep—perhaps all because her hand had touched his, or because she had spoken some word to him that had possessed him with a ravishing disquietude?

All this might not have befallen him had Sir John Malyoe looked after his granddaughter instead of locking himself up day and night in his own cabin, scarce venturing out except to devour his food or maybe to take two or three turns across the deck before returning again to the care of those chests he appeared to hold so much more precious than his own flesh and blood.

Nor was it to be supposed that Barnaby would take the pains to consider what was to become of it all, for what young man so situated as he but would be perfectly content to live so agreeably in a fool's paradise, satisfying himself by assigning the whole affair to the future to take care of itself. Accordingly, our hero endeavored, and with pretty good success, to put away from him whatever doubts might arise in his own mind concerning what he was about, satisfying himself with making his conversation as agreeable to his companion as it lay in his power to do.

So the affair continued until the end of the whole business came with a suddenness that promised for a time to cast our hero into the utmost depths of humiliation and despair.

At that time the *Belle Helen* was, according to Captain Manly's reckoning, computed that day at noon, bearing about five-and-fifty leagues northeast-by-east off the harbor of Charleston, in South Carolina.

Nor was our hero likely to forget for many years afterwards even the smallest circumstance of that occasion. He may remember that it was a mightily sweet, balmy evening, the sun not having set above half an hour before, and the sky still suffused with a good deal of brightness, the air being extremely soft and mild. He may remember with the utmost nicety